The Inner Circle

A CHAOS COVEN PREQUEL

CARLY BRYANT

For more information, contact: **http://www.carlybwrites.com**

Cover Design: GetCovers.com
Editor: Jaime Tragesser

ISBN: Paperback – 979-8-9997052-9

First Edition: February 2026

Contents

Where It All Began

Before the photographs. Before the coffee shop. Before Sierra Turner figured out that being truly seen could feel like something other than a warning.

The Inner Circle is the story I had to write first. The one that shows you who these people are to each other before everything else gets complicated. You don't need it to read Loving Lauren, but if you want to understand the foundation, this is it.

If you're brand new here, welcome. This story stands on its own. But when you're ready for what comes next, Sierra and Lauren's full love story is waiting for you in Loving Lauren.

If you've already read it? Now you know what they were like before.

Either way, I'm really glad you're here.

With love,
Carly

Content Warnings

Your mental health is important to me. Please see the list of content warnings.

- References to bullying
- Grief and loss (death of a family member)
- Family rejection
- Panic attacks and anxiety
- Toxic family dynamics
- Physical altercations / interpersonal conflict
- Mild sexual content (not explicit)
- Alcohol use (minor, social)
- Transgender character representation

Before Everything Changed

Sierra

B**EFORE EVERYTHING CHANGED, S**IERRA thought loneliness was something people eventually outgrew. Like acne. Or awkward phases. Or the weird need to pretend you liked people you barely tolerated to survive high school.

She did not know then that some kinds of loneliness stayed put until the right people cracked them open. She did not know that years later, love would walk into her life and shift everything she thought she understood about herself.

Back then, she was sixteen and sitting in an art classroom that smelled like turpentine, chalk dust, and possibility.

Junior Year

Mr. Brennan had arranged the still life at the front of the

room with a seriousness most people saved for funerals and weddings. A ceramic vase. Three apples. A length of fabric draped over a stool in dramatic folds that were probably meant to look elegant, though to Sierra it looked more like somebody had raided their grandmother's linen closet and called it inspiration.

She was supposed to be sketching that.

She was not.

Instead, charcoal moved between her fingers in quick, sure strokes, shaping the profile of the girl seated two rows over. Sharp eyeliner. Dark hair. A face that looked like it had mastered the art of daring the world to try something stupid. There was something magnetic about her, something self-contained and unbothered.

"That's really good."

Sierra startled so hard she nearly dragged the side of her hand through the drawing.

A redheaded girl from the next table had leaned into her space without warning, green eyes bright with an interest that felt genuine instead of nosy.

The girl pointed at the page. "I mean it. You somehow made Raven look interesting. No offense to still life, but those apples are boring as hell."

Sierra's gaze flicked up to the dark-haired girl she had been drawing. Raven, apparently. Raven had turned in her seat and was looking back at them with mild curiosity, as if being sketched by a stranger ranked somewhere between mildly flattering and not worth making a fuss over.

"I'm Calliope," the redhead said, not bothering to lower her voice even though Mr. Brennan had already started eyeing their section with suspicion. "You're Sierra, right?"

"Yeah." Sierra tucked a loose strand of blonde hair behind her ear and tried not to look too thrown.

Calliope studied her. "You always sit alone at lunch."

Not mean. Not pitying. Just factual.

That somehow made it worse.

Sierra shrugged, because there did not seem to be a cool way to answer that. "I don't know. Easier, I guess."

"Easier than what?" Raven asked, pivoting fully in her seat now. "Talking to people?"

Sierra opened her mouth, then closed it.

Raven lifted one shoulder. "That's depressing."

"Raven doesn't believe in small talk or subtlety," Calliope said cheerfully. "You should know that before you get attached."

Mr. Brennan cleared his throat from the front of the room.

All three of them bent over their work with exaggerated innocence nobody actually bought. Silence stretched for maybe half a minute before Calliope leaned over again and whispered, "Sit with us at lunch. You draw people like you actually see them. I need that energy in my life."

Sierra almost laughed, mostly because she was not sure how else to react.

She also almost said no.

No was easy. No was familiar. No meant going back to the quiet corner she usually claimed in the cafeteria, picking at fries, and pretending solitude was a choice instead of a habit that had hardened into armor.

But before she could offer some excuse about homework or plans or needing to reorganize her locker for the fifth time that week, Raven cut in.

She smiled. "It's not really a request. Calli's already decided. You might as well accept your fate."

For a second, Sierra just stared at them.

Then, somehow, against every instinct she had spent years carefully building, she nodded.

She nodded, and the air between them changed.

THE CAFETERIA WAS LOUD in the way only high school cafeterias could be. Chairs scraped. Someone shouted across the room. Trays clattered. The air smelled like fryer grease, ketchup, and whatever chemical substance passed for pizza sauce in public schools.

Sierra followed Calliope and Raven to a corner table by the windows, the one most people avoided because the sunlight hit it all wrong. Too bright. Too exposed. No shadows to hide in.

"Perfect lighting," Sierra murmured before she could stop herself.

Calliope dropped her lunch tray onto the table with a loud clatter and pointed at her like she had proven a major scientific theory. "See? She gets it. Raven, she gets it."

"I noticed." Raven sat down and pulled a black plastic container from her bag. Inside was some kind of rice dish so aggressively dark it looked like it had been conjured by a sea witch. "My mom is on a squid ink kick. Want to try some?"

Sierra eyed it. "Is that safe?"

"Probably." Raven took a bite, chewed, then made a face that answered the question better than words could. "Debatable."

Calliope snorted.

To Sierra's surprise, conversation came easier than she expected.

Calliope talked fast and with her whole body, telling them about a piece of fanfiction she had been reading during library period until she laughed so hard the librarian kicked her out.

"It was discrimination," she said. "You cannot punish a girl for having standards and a sense of humor."

Raven, with far more dignity than the moment deserved, produced a tarot deck from her backpack and began shuffling with quiet concentration.

"I'm learning," she said. "So far the cards mostly think everyone is doomed."

"That tracks," Calliope said.

Sierra listened more than she talked at first, soaking in the strange ease of it all. There was no audition here. No moment where she had to prove she was interesting enough or funny enough or loud enough to earn a place at the table. They just kept making room for her, as if it had already been decided.

Her breathing steadied.

Without really thinking about it, she reached into her bag and pulled out her camera.

Her parents had found it secondhand for her birthday the year before. It had a scratch along the side and a lens cap that liked to fall off at inconvenient times, but Sierra loved it with a kind of devotion that bordered on embarrassing. Through it, things arranged themselves into something legible. Manageable. Beautiful, even.

She lifted it and framed the table.

Click.

Calliope mid-laugh, one hand still in the air.

Click.

Raven with her tarot cards spread between her fingers like she was about to summon a spirit in the middle of lunch period.

Click.

Sunlight washing across both of their faces, too bright for anyone else and somehow perfect to Sierra.

Through the viewfinder, the world made sense.

Then Calliope stopped talking so abruptly it took Sierra a second to notice.

"Okay," Calliope said slowly, eyes fixed somewhere over Sierra's shoulder, "do not turn around, but Brad Dickhead is currently shoving somebody into a locker."

Sierra turned around immediately.

At the far wall, a skinny boy with warm brown skin and narrow shoulders was being folded into a locker by three grinning jocks who looked delighted with themselves. He was trying, very hard, not to let them see he was upset. That somehow made it worse. When they finally laughed and walked off, he stayed crammed in there for another few seconds before pulling himself free with stiff, humiliated movements.

Sierra lowered the camera.

Her chest tightened.

"That's Jett," Raven said, quieter now. "He's in my English class."

"He okay?" Sierra asked, though the answer was obvious.

Raven gave her a look. "No. He's definitely not okay."

Calliope's usual brightness had dimmed. "Brad's a nightmare. Administration doesn't care. Half the staff acts like being cruel is just boys being boys."

Sierra watched Jett crouch to gather his dropped papers. His movements had a careful, practiced quality to them, like he had learned how to make himself smaller when people got mean.

"We should do something," she said.

Calliope looked at her. "Like what?"

Sierra did not have an answer.

Raven drummed her fingers on the table once, thinking. "We could invite him over here."

Sierra glanced back at her. "That's it?"

"Why not?" Raven said. "We're clearly already the island of misfit toys."

"The island of misfit queers," Calliope corrected, leaning back in her chair. "At least let us brand accurately."

Sierra's heart gave a strange little jolt.

The way Calliope said it was so casual. So unashamed.

Like it was not a confession or a risk. Just a fact.

Calliope caught her expression and softened a little. "I'm a lesbian, in case that helps. Raven is still figuring some things out."

"Questioning," Raven said. "Which feels annoyingly vague, but there it is."

Then both of them looked at Sierra.

Patient. Open. Waiting.

Her throat tightened.

Nobody had ever asked her like that before, as if there was room for whatever her answer might be.

"I don't know," she admitted quietly. "Not exactly. But I know I'm not straight."

Calliope grinned like Sierra had passed some invisible test. "Good enough for me."

Raven nodded once. "Same."

Saying it aloud rewired something. The air felt charged.

Calliope glanced back at Jett. "Cool. Then yes, we should absolutely adopt the terrified gay kid. Safety in numbers."

THE NEXT DAY, RAVEN arrived at lunch with Jett trailing behind her like she had, in fact, simply scooped him up and brought him there by force.

"New recruit," she announced, nudging him toward the empty chair. "Jett, meet Sierra and Calliope. Ladies, this is Jett. He's one of us."

"Jesus, Raven," Calliope said, already grinning, "let him breathe."

Jett stood there for half a second too long, shoulders tense, backpack strap clutched in one hand like he might need to make a run for it.

Sierra smiled at him, hoping it looked warm instead of painfully awkward. "I'm Sierra. I've seen you around."

His face changed just enough to tell her that helped. "You're in my English class."

"I know." She almost added, *You draw in the margins of your notebook when you're bored*, but that sounded like the kind of thing that got people labeled creepy, so she kept it to herself.

Calliope stuck out a hand. "Calliope. You can call me Calli unless you annoy me."

Jett let out a startled little laugh and shook it.

That was all it took.

The tension in his shoulders eased enough for him to sit.

Calliope rested her chin in her hand and studied him like he was the newest addition to a reality show she fully intended to produce. "So. What's your story? Closeted baby gay, fully out and thriving, or somewhere in the deeply unfortunate middle where most of us are currently rotting?"

Jett looked at Raven, who only shrugged as if to say, yes, this is your life now.

"I came out to my mom last month," he said after a moment. "She was... actually really good about it."

All three of them reacted at once.

"Wait, seriously?"

"No screaming?"

"No dramatic church pamphlets?"

Jett laughed for real that time, and it changed his whole face. "No. She just hugged me. Then she asked if I was okay and if I wanted takeout."

Calliope clutched her chest. "The dream."

"My mom knows," Calliope added. "She asked if this meant she'd eventually get a daughter-in-law with excellent taste in wine. Which is a weird thing to say to your teenage daughter, but I respected the energy."

"My parents don't know," Sierra said, the words slipping out before she could stop them. "I'm not sure they'd understand."

The table went quiet in a way that felt gentle instead of awkward.

"My parents are in denial," Raven said. "They keep talking about when I meet the right guy, which is bold of them considering I barely want to meet the right people."

That earned a snort from Calliope.

"We're all disasters," she declared. "Welcome to the dysfunctional family you did not ask for but very clearly need."

Jett ducked his head, smiling, and something in his face opened. Sierra saw it happen in real time. The careful, braced version of him loosened. Like he had been waiting for the room to turn hostile and was slowly realizing it would not.

Lunch turned into after school.

After school turned into every day after that.

The four of them developed a rhythm so naturally it felt almost suspicious. Calliope talked enough for three people. Raven supplied dry commentary from the sidelines. Jett slowly revealed a wicked sense of humor. Sierra kept bringing her camera everywhere, documenting all of it in stolen little flashes.

Click.

Calliope laughing so hard soda nearly came out of her nose.

Click.

Raven reading tarot for people in the hallway like a goth oracle on break.

Click.

Jett smiling in a way that no longer looked fragile.

Behind the camera, everything felt steadier.

Her friends made sense. She made sense. The world finally felt like something she could step into instead of stand outside and watch.

When Calliope created a group chat and named it **The Chaos Coven**, Sierra saved the first screenshot immediately.

Not because it was especially funny, though it was.

Because some part of her needed proof.

Proof that this was real. Proof that she had not imagined them. Proof that she belonged somewhere at last.

THAT NIGHT, SIERRA LAY sprawled across her bed with Salem stretched over her stomach like a possessive, purring furnace. He was still small enough to be all limbs and ears, but he carried himself with the confidence of a tiny dictator. She scratched absently behind one velvet-soft ear and stared up at the wall across from her.

Posters. Band flyers. A few photography prints she had begged her mom to let her frame properly. Jensen Ackles. Emma Watson.

Her bedroom door opened a crack.

Tobias leaned into her room. "Mom wants us downstairs in ten."

"Okay."

He did not leave right away.

Instead, his gaze drifted to her wall, and he nodded toward the Emma Watson poster with easy teenage-boy certainty. "Dude. Emma Watson is so hot."

Sierra froze.

Her fingers stilled in Salem's fur.

"Yeah," she said automatically.

Then her own answer hit her.

Yeah.

Not in the vague, objective way people were supposed to admire celebrities. Not in the same way someone might acknowledge that a sunset was pretty, or a painting was well done.

No, she meant it the way Tobias meant it.

Her pulse skidded.

Because she also meant it the way she meant Jensen Ackles.

For one strange, suspended second, it felt like the world had tilted an inch off its axis.

"You okay?" Tobias asked.

"Yeah." She forced a shrug. "Just tired."

He gave her a look that said he did not entirely buy that, but he let it go. "Don't take forever. Mom's already in one of her moods."

When he left, Sierra stared at the poster in silence.

Emma Watson's smile. The flutter in Sierra's chest. The memory of the girl in her math class whose laugh always made her look up.

Salem chirped and kneaded once against her stomach, demanding she resume the petting he had clearly been promised.

She obeyed automatically, her thoughts still racing.

She liked girls.

Not just in an abstract way. Not just in a *they're pretty, I want to look like that* kind of way.

She liked girls.

And she liked boys.

Josh from chemistry made her stomach flip every time he smiled at her. Emma Watson did too. So did the girl in math with the silver nose ring. So did a whole list of possibilities Sierra had not let herself name before now.

"What does that make me?" she whispered to Salem.

Salem blinked at her with the profound indifference of a cat who had no interest in human sexuality as long as dinner happened on time.

A laugh escaped her before she could stop it.

She still did not have the words. Not fully. Not neatly. But the panic she might have expected never quite arrived.

Maybe that was because of the texts lighting up her phone on the nightstand.

Calliope had changed the group chat icon three times in an hour. Raven was threatening murder. Jett had sent a picture of his homework with the caption *help me, I am perishing*. The screen kept glowing every few seconds with proof that somewhere in the city, three people were already making room for her in their lives.

She had found her people.

And maybe that should have felt like the end of something. Maybe it should have made her feel finished, settled, complete.

Instead, lying there with Salem purring against her ribs and her friends lighting up the dark from the other side of her phone, Sierra felt the shape of something else too. Something unnamed. A space inside her she still had not figured out how to fill.

Maybe someday she would find the right words for herself.

Maybe someday she would understand why her heart still felt like it was waiting for something.

But not yet.

Not then.

Before everything changed, this was enough.

The Name They Chose

Lauren

Before everything changed, Lauren believed survival meant making yourself small enough that no one would notice you at all.

If you stayed quiet, stayed agreeable, stayed invisible, maybe the world would let you exist without asking too many questions. Maybe you could get through high school, get out, and finally become someone real somewhere far away.

They didn't know yet that love would one day demand the opposite. That someone would look at them and see everything they had been trying so hard to hide.

Back then, they were sixteen and standing in their bedroom, staring at clothes that felt like a costume they were required to wear.

Junior Year

Navy polo shirt. Khaki pants. The uniform of not drawing attention.

Lauren touched the fabric with their fingertips. It was stiff. Structured. Wrong in a way that went deeper than comfort or style. It felt like wearing someone else's skin.

What they wanted was buried in the back of the closet, hidden inside a garbage bag behind winter coats their mother never moved. A single thrifted dress. Soft, flowing, light enough to make them feel like they could breathe.

Three dollars. Purchased with crumpled cash and a pounding heart.

Wearing it would mean questions. Questions would mean confrontation. Confrontation would mean losing what little peace existed in the house.

Not yet.

They pulled on the polo shirt and tried not to feel like they were disappearing inside it.

M R. Lear's classroom during lunch had become their refuge.

Mr. Lear caught them hiding in there. "You three can use this room. Just don't burn anything down."

So now they arrived early, before the hallways filled, before anyone could see where Lauren disappeared during lunch.

Willow was already there, perched cross-legged on a desk, a compact mirror balanced in one hand. She reapplied lipstick with the confidence of someone who had earned the right to take up space.

Willow glanced up. "Hey. You're late."

"Had to wait for the hallway to clear." Lauren dropped their backpack and pulled out their phone. "Couldn't risk anyone seeing me come in here."

Willow's expression softened immediately. She understood. She always understood.

Willow had come out years earlier. Her parents had helped her transition, helped her pick clothes, and helped her learn makeup. She moved through the world like it belonged to her.

Lauren's parents preferred to pretend the problem did not exist.

"What are you watching?" Willow peeked at their phone.

"NikkieTutorials." Lauren angled the phone toward her. "She makes it look so easy. Like being trans doesn't have to mean being miserable."

"She's incredible," Willow said. "Have you seen her..."

The door burst open, and Jordan entered with arms full of vending machine loot.

Jordan beamed. "I bring offerings. Also the machine ate my dollar, so we're all emotionally invested in these Takis now."

"You're a goddess." Willow grabbed a bag.

Jordan tossed another to Lauren with a grin. She had been Lauren's friend since freshman year. Fierce, blunt, and loyal in a way that felt almost reckless. When Willow came out, Jordan had just asked what pronouns to use and moved on. When Lauren started showing up with eyeliner, she didn't blink.

Lauren pulled out their own makeup bag. It was small and carefully curated from drugstore purchases made in secret. Each item felt precious, fragile, and dangerous.

"You doing a full face?" Jordan asked.

"Just eyeliner. Maybe gloss." Lauren steadied their hands as they uncapped the liner. "I've been practicing."

Willow slid closer. "Let me see."

Lauren drew a careful line along their lash line, holding their breath the entire time. When they finished, they checked the result on their phone camera.

Not perfect.

But closer.

Willow turned to look at them. "You're getting really good."

"You look good." Jordan's tone was gentler than usual.

Lauren swallowed. "I feel good."

The words slipped out before they could stop them.

They fidgeted with the eyeliner pen, then glanced at both of them. "You guys ever wonder why I picked Lauren?"

Willow and Jordan exchanged a look.

"We figured you'd tell us when you were ready," Willow said.

"It's your name," Jordan said simply. "That's enough."

"It's important to me." Lauren took a breath that shook on the way out. "My grandpa used to talk about this actress he loved when he was younger. Lauren Bacall. He'd do this terrible impression of her voice just to make my grandma laugh."

They smiled faintly at the memory.

"He's the only one who never made me feel like I was broken. He treated me like me." Their voice wavered. "I wanted a name that came from someone who actually loves me."

Willow's eyes softened. "That's beautiful."

"Old Hollywood energy," Jordan said. "Very classy."

Lauren laughed weakly. "And they/them feels better lately. Like it fits. Not exactly girl, but definitely not what everyone else thinks."

"It suits you," Willow said.

"You seem less tense," Jordan added. "Like you're not waiting for someone to yell at you."

Lauren looked at their reflection again. The eyeliner. The gloss. The person on the screen looked closer to real than anything they saw at home.

Everything felt steady.

Then the classroom door opened.

THE OFFICE AIDE SCANNED the room until her gaze landed on Lauren.

"Your parents are here to pick you up."

Lauren's stomach dropped.

They never came to school.

"Why?"

The aide shook her head. "They didn't say."

Willow squeezed Lauren's hand. Jordan stood like she was ready to throw punches.

"It's probably nothing," Lauren said, though their voice had already begun to shake.

They shoved the makeup bag deep into their backpack and wiped frantically at their face. No mirror. No way to know if they had erased enough.

"Text us," Willow said.

Lauren nodded.

The walk to the office felt endless.

Their parents were waiting. Mom's eyes were red. Dad's jaw tight.

For a second, Lauren thought maybe Mom would hug them.

Instead, her gaze landed on Lauren's face.

Disgust replaced grief.

"Are you wearing makeup?" she demanded.

Lauren wanted the floor to open and swallow them whole.

"In the car," Dad said quietly. "Now."

T HE DOORS SHUT.

The engine started.

Mom turned around in her seat.

"Your grandfather died this morning."

The words didn't land. They hovered, meaningless.

"What?"

"Heart attack. He's gone."

Gone.

The only adult who had never looked at them like a problem to solve. The only person who called them kiddo with warmth instead of disappointment.

"And you couldn't even." Mom gestured at their face. "You couldn't be normal for one day."

Lauren scrubbed at their eyes. The eyeliner smeared. They didn't care anymore.

"He loved you," Mom said, her voice sharp with grief and anger. "And this is how you show up?"

Lauren pressed their hands to their face and cried.

In their backpack, their phone buzzed.

> Willow: Are you okay?

> Jordan: What happened??

> Willow: We're here if you need us. Lauren.

Their name.

The one chosen from love. The one their grandfather would have understood without question.

Lauren clung to it like a life raft.

Everything else might be falling apart. But this one thing was theirs. Untouchable. Real.

Before everything changed, that was enough to survive.

The Things She Couldn't Name

Sierra

BEFORE EVERYTHING CHANGED, SIERRA thought *wanting* was supposed to be simple.

You liked someone. They liked you back if you were lucky. You went on dates, had first kisses, learned the shape of ordinary happiness. That was how it worked in movies, in books, in hallway gossip whispered between classes.

She did not know yet that desire could split open in more than one direction. That a person could feel right and still not be the whole answer. That sometimes the most confusing thing in the world was not heartbreak, but being happy and still sensing there was more.

Back then, she was sixteen and trying very hard not to stare at the back of Josh Martinez's neck during chemistry.

Junior Year

It was not going well.

He sat two rows ahead of her, slightly off to the left, which was somehow the perfect angle for distraction. That day he was wearing a faded band T-shirt under his school hoodie, and his hair looked like he had either woken up late or run his hands through it a hundred times without noticing. Every few seconds, he tilted his head while concentrating on the board, and each time he did, Sierra forgot whatever Mr. Reynolds was saying about covalent bonds.

She had written exactly half a sentence in her notebook.

Calliope leaned toward Sierra. "You're staring again."

Sierra jerked her gaze down so fast she nearly dropped her pencil. "I'm not."

"You are. It's honestly painful to witness at this point."

"I was looking past him."

"At the wall?"

Sierra kept her eyes on her notebook. "Maybe the wall is interesting."

Calliope made a muted, unconvinced sound. "Just talk to him already."

"And say what? Hi, I've been admiring you for weeks?"

Calliope pressed a hand dramatically to her chest. "God, that's incredible. You should absolutely say that."

Sierra bit back a laugh, which turned into a weird

half-snort. Mr. Reynolds glanced in their direction. She ducked her head and pretended sudden fascination with her notes.

The bell rang twenty minutes later, and Sierra packed up slowly on purpose, pretending to reorganize papers she had already organized twice. She was not sure whether or not she wanted Josh to notice her. Wanting something and being terrified of it seemed to be her entire personality, lately.

He noticed her.

"Hey, Sierra, right?"

She looked up so fast that her backpack strap slipped off her shoulder.

Josh stood there with one hand hooked around his bag, his expression open and a little nervous, which somehow made him even cuter.

"Yeah," she said, then winced inwardly at how breathless it sounded. "Hi."

"I know we haven't really talked much." He rubbed the back of his neck. "There's a photography exhibit down-town this weekend. I remembered you always have your camera, so I thought maybe you'd want to go?"

For one bright, suspended second, Sierra forgot how to speak.

He had noticed her camera.

He had noticed her.

Calliope, now shamelessly lingering by the door, made a tiny choking noise that might have been excitement and might have been her trying not to laugh.

"Yes," Sierra said quickly. "I mean, yeah. I'd love that."

Josh's smile was warm and a little relieved. "Cool. I'll text you?"

She nodded.

He left, and Sierra remained standing there like her soul had briefly exited her body and not fully returned.

The second she stepped into the hallway, Calliope grabbed both her arms.

"Oh my God."

"He asked me out," Sierra whispered, as if saying it too loudly might somehow undo it.

"I gathered that from the part where he asked you out."

Sierra laughed then, helpless and giddy and a little stunned. Calliope threw an arm around her shoulders and marched her toward lunch like they were heading to announce a royal engagement.

BY THE TIME THEY reached the cafeteria, Raven and Jett were already at their usual table.

Raven looked up first. "Why do you look like you've just seen God?"

"Josh asked me out."

Calliope gestured at Sierra. "This is history. This is a monumental day. You have entered your dating era."

Raven raised an eyebrow at Sierra. "You said yes?"

"Yes."

"Good," Raven said. "He seems normal."

"That is such a bleak endorsement," Jett said.

"It is high praise coming from me."

Sierra dropped into her seat, trying and failing to stop smiling. "He asked me to go to this photography exhibit downtown."

Jett leaned forward. "That's actually adorable."

"See?" Calliope said. "He pays attention. This is promising. We need to discuss outfit options immediately."

"We do not," Sierra said.

"We absolutely do. This is your first real date. We need strategy."

Raven opened her lunch container and looked deeply unimpressed by the entire concept of strategy. "Her strategy should be to go and talk like a normal person."

"Some of us do not come by normal person behavior naturally, Raven."

"That is true."

Sierra laughed, then glanced down at her tray. Her stomach felt too full of nerves to eat much of anything.

Jett noticed. "You okay?"

"Yeah. Just... kind of freaking out."

"In a good way?" he asked.

"In a terrifying way that is mostly good."

"That's how you know it matters," Calliope said.

Sierra thought about that longer than she meant to.

It did matter. Josh mattered, at least in the bright, new way crushes mattered when you were sixteen and every possibility still felt enormous. He was sweet. Funny in a low-key way that caught her off guard. The kind of boy her parents would instantly approve of, which should not have mattered, but did.

Maybe because approval made things simpler.

Maybe because simple sounded nice.

"You going to tell your parents?" Jett asked.

Sierra picked at the edge of her napkin. "I guess I have to, but I don't know. It's just one date."

Calliope gave her a look over the top of her juice box. "It is never just one date when you stare at someone like you're writing poetry with your eyeballs."

Sierra buried her face in her hands.

"Oh my God," Raven said flatly. "She's blushing."

"I hate all of you."

"No, you don't," Jett said.

He was right.

THE WEEKEND CAME FASTER than Sierra was ready for.

She changed outfits three times before settling on jeans, boots, and a sweater that Calliope had declared made her look "effortlessly cool but still dateable," which sounded fake but was apparently a compliment.

When Josh arrived, he was right on time.

He smiled when Sierra opened the door, and something in her chest turned over.

"You look really nice," he said.

Her face warmed instantly. "You too."

He took her downtown on the subway, and by the time they reached the exhibit, some of her nerves had softened into excitement. The gallery occupied the second floor of an old brick building with massive windows and polished concrete floors. Everything smelled faintly of dust, coffee from the shop downstairs, and expensive paper.

The photographs lined the walls in careful rows. Some were huge and dramatic, all shadows and bone structure and impossible beauty. Others were quieter. A woman smoking alone on a fire escape. A little boy with a scraped knee standing in a summer sprinkler. An empty church pew in a flood of afternoon light.

Sierra stopped in front of one black-and-white portrait and stayed there longer than she meant to.

The subject was an older man, his face weathered and unsmiling, but his hands were folded so gently in his lap that the whole image softened around them. There was an entire life in those hands. A marriage, maybe. Regret. Tenderness. Grief.

Josh stepped up beside her. "You always look at pictures like they're about to tell you a secret."

Sierra glanced at him. "That's because the good ones do."

He smiled. "See, that. That's what I mean."

"What?"

"You don't just look at things. You look through them." He nodded toward the portrait. "I saw an old guy in a chair. You saw a whole story."

Sierra tucked a strand of hair behind her ear. "That's what makes it interesting. The story behind it."

He looked at her then instead of the photo, and his expression changed in some small but unmistakable way.

"Yeah," he said quietly.

The rest of the afternoon passed in easy, surprising conversation. They talked about the exhibit, obviously, but also music and teachers they hated and whether Brooklyn bagels were genuinely better than every other bagel in existence or if New Yorkers were just unbearable about bread. Josh made her laugh twice so hard she had to stop walking. At one point, he held open a gallery door for her with a stupidly formal little bow that should have been corny but somehow was not.

Afterward, they got hot chocolate from a café down the block and stood outside talking until the air turned colder and the sky went lavender around the buildings.

When he walked her home later, Sierra's heart began pounding so hard she could feel it in her throat.

They stopped beneath a streetlight washed in orange.

Josh shoved his hands into his jacket pockets, then took one back out almost immediately, as if he had thought better of trying to act casual. "I had a really good time."

"Me too."

Her voice came out softer than she intended.

He stepped a little closer. "Can I kiss you?"

She nodded.

His hand came up gently, fingers resting against her jaw like he was afraid to move too fast. The kiss itself was sweet and a little clumsy and warm with leftover hot chocolate.

Sierra's fingers caught in the front of his jacket because her knees suddenly felt unreliable and she did not know where else to put her hands.

It was her first real kiss.

Not the idea of one. Not the kind she had imagined during boring classes or while listening to songs that made everything feel cinematic. An actual kiss, happening to her, right there under a Brooklyn streetlight while the city moved around them like it had no idea anything important had just happened.

When he pulled back, he was smiling.

So was she.

For a few seconds, the whole world narrowed to that.

Then Josh laughed under his breath, almost shy. "Okay. Good. I'm glad I did that."

Sierra laughed too, relief and joy tangling together in her chest. "Me too."

S HE FLOATED UPSTAIRS.

There was really no other word for it.

She closed her bedroom door behind her, leaned against it, and stood there grinning at nothing for a full minute. Salem looked up from the bed and gave her the kind of slow blink that suggested he found human drama exhausting.

"It happened," she told him, crossing the room. "An actual kiss happened."

Salem meowed once, which she decided to interpret as supportive.

She changed into pajamas, crawled into bed, and replayed the whole evening in her mind from start to finish. The gallery. The hot chocolate. The way Josh had looked at her, like what she said mattered. The softness of his mouth. The little jolt in her stomach when he touched her face.

It had been perfect.

Or close enough to perfect that the difference did not matter.

Sierra could not explain why, but as she lay there in the dark, another thought kept brushing the edge of everything good.

Not that something was wrong.

Nothing was wrong.

Only that there might be more.

More feeling. More wanting. More to understand about herself than one sweet kiss under one streetlight could answer.

THE FOLLOWING FRIDAY, THE Coven sprawled across Calliope's basement in their usual chaotic arrangement of limbs, pizza boxes, and commentary. A horror movie played while Calliope offered loudly incorrect predictions about every possible ending.

Sierra was midway through telling them about her date with Josh when her thoughts snagged on something from earlier that day.

A girl she did not know had held the door open for her in the hallway that morning. Dark curls, silver hoops, a smile quick and easy and gone almost as soon as it appeared.

Sierra had thanked her and kept walking.

Then spent the next ten minutes thinking about the fact that her stomach had flipped the exact same way it did when Josh smiled at her.

"You okay?" Jett asked.

Sierra blinked. "Yeah. Sorry. Just got distracted."

Calliope narrowed her eyes. "Distracted how?"

"Nothing."

"That is never true when people say it like that."

Sierra threw a balled-up napkin at her. Calliope dodged it with a triumphant cackle.

The conversation rolled on, but part of Sierra stayed snagged on that stupid hallway moment. On the girl in art class, she sometimes caught herself noticing. On the barista at the coffee shop near school, whose smile always lingered a second too long in Sierra's head afterward. On the fact that none of those things canceled out how much she liked Josh.

If anything, that was what made it more confusing.

She liked him. Really liked him.

So why did the rest of it still feel so alive inside her, too?

THAT NIGHT, SIERRA LAY in bed with Salem tucked against her side, his purr loud enough to vibrate through the mattress. She scratched beneath his chin and stared up at the ceiling.

She liked Josh.

That much was easy.

But easy was not the same thing as complete.

Every glance and flutter and momentary spark had lodged itself somewhere under her skin, not as a replacement for Josh, but as a truth standing beside him.

She scratched Salem's jaw. "What does it mean if you like boys and girls?"

Salem chirped and kneaded her blanket with unnecessary intensity.

"Thanks. Super insightful."

He headbutted her wrist and demanded more attention.

Sierra obliged, her thoughts still spinning.

"I think I'm different. Not bad different. Just different."

And maybe that was why the coven felt so necessary. Calliope with her certainty. Raven with her questioning. Jett with the brave, matter-of-fact way he claimed himself even when the world made that hard.

Sierra did not know what label fit yet. She did not know if she was ready for one. But the panic she might have expected never fully came.

Maybe because she was not trying to figure it out alone.

Her phone buzzed on the nightstand.

> **Josh:** Had a really great time on our date. Want to do it again soon?

Sierra smiled before she could help it and typed back a yes.

A second later, another notification lit up the screen.

The Chaos Coven

> **Calliope:** Friday movie night at my place next week. Horror marathon. Mandatory.

Jett: I'm bringing snacks and my winning personality.

Raven: Your personality has never won anything.

Calliope: Sierra, bring your camera. We need documentation in case Jett dies dramatically.

Sierra laughed softly. She had people who saw her even when she was still learning how to see herself.

She set the phone down and looked at Salem.

"A girl who likes a boy, and probably girls too."

Salem blinked.

"A girl who's figuring it out."

That still felt true.

More true, maybe, than anything else.

She closed her eyes and let herself rest inside that uncertainty instead of fighting it. It was not as frightening as it had been before.

Not with the coven, and with proof she was not alone. Not with a life that was beginning, little by little, to feel like hers.

Before everything changed, this was enough, too.

The First Place They Could Breathe

Lauren

B EFORE EVERYTHING CHANGED, LAUREN learned that grief could strip a person down to whatever truth they had been avoiding.

Sometimes loss did not make people softer. Sometimes it made them honest. Sometimes it left nothing but the unbearable weight of what could no longer be postponed.

By the time of the funeral, Lauren already knew hiding was killing something inside them. They just had not known yet that one terrible day would force the rest of it into the open.

Back then, they were sixteen, dressed like a stranger, and standing in the third pew while the wrong life was being mourned right alongside their grandfather.

Junior Year

The funeral director kept using the wrong name for them without ever saying it outright.

Lauren stood in stiff khakis and a button-down shirt that felt like a straightjacket, listening to a stranger talk about their grandfather in a polished funeral-home voice.

Beloved husband. Devoted father. Proud grandfather to his grandson.

Grandchild! Lauren wanted to scream.

Not grandson. Never grandson.

But their mouth stayed shut.

They stood there in borrowed grief clothes, shoulders tight, collar scratching at their neck, and tried not to come apart while the only person who had ever loved them without conditions lay in a casket at the front of the room.

Their mother cried quietly into a tissue. Their father kept one arm around her shoulders, jaw set in that grim, rigid way that always meant he was holding himself together through force alone. Around them, aunts and uncles and cousins filled the pews in black, all of them performing grief in the approved family way.

Lauren felt numb at first.

Then not numb at all.

They felt everything. The pinch of their shoes. The sweat gathering beneath the collar of their shirt. The weight of every glance that slid their way when someone said grandson again. The humiliation of standing there as a version of themselves they had never chosen. The certainty that their grandfather would have hated every second of it.

Not the grief. Not yet.

But the performance. The stiffness. The way Lauren had been buttoned into someone else's skin for the comfort of everyone else in the room.

After the service, people came at them in waves.

"He was so proud of you."

"You look just like him."

"Such a handsome young man."

Each one landed like a small, clean cut.

Lauren accepted hugs they did not want and nodded through words that made them want to disappear. They kept their face blank because that was easier than letting anyone see what was really happening under their skin.

By the time they got home, the numbness had curdled into something hot and restless.

THE HOUSE FILLED QUICKLY.

Relatives drifted through the kitchen and living room with casseroles, paper plates, soft voices, and the strange appetite people always seemed to develop after funerals. Someone put on coffee. Someone else opened the fridge and started rearranging leftovers as if organizing someone else's kitchen counted as comfort.

Lauren slipped upstairs before anyone could stop them.

The second their bedroom door shut, they stripped off the funeral clothes.

The button-down hit the floor first. Then the khakis. Then the belt they had wanted to rip off since noon.

They sat on the edge of the bed in boxers and an undershirt, breathing hard, staring at the closet.

At the back of it.

At the garbage bag hidden behind winter coats and old blankets.

Downstairs, voices drifted up through the vents.

Your kid handled today so well.

So mature.

Your father would've been proud.

Proud.

The word hollowed them out.

Would he have been proud of this?

Of Lauren standing there in clothes that made them want to crawl out of their own body? Of sitting quietly while a room full of people described a grandson who did not exist? Of swallowing every truth until it turned sharp inside them?

No.

Their grandfather had never been that kind of man.

He had not understood everything, maybe. Lauren was old enough now to know that love and understanding were not always identical things. But he had looked at them with warmth. With curiosity. With something far closer to acceptance than anything else in their life. He had made space for them without demanding an explanation. He had loved first and figured the rest out later.

And now he was gone.

Lauren stood so suddenly that the bedframe creaked.

They crossed the room, shoved aside the coats, and dragged out the garbage bag with shaking hands.

Inside was the dress.

Pale blue. Thrifted. Soft enough to feel unreal.

They had only worn it twice before, both times in the dead center of the night while the house slept around them. Both times they had stood in front of the mirror and felt something inside them click painfully, beautifully into place.

Like recognition.

Like meeting themselves in secret.

They pulled it on now with hands that would not quite steady. The fabric skimmed their body differently than boys' clothes did. It moved when they moved. It made them feel visible instead of erased.

At the desk, they opened their makeup bag.

Foundation. Concealer. A soft line of eyeliner. A muted lipstick.

Nothing dramatic. Nothing theatrical. Just enough to make the person in the mirror feel possible.

When they finished, they looked up.

Lauren looked back.

Not the grandson from the funeral program. Not the child in the family photos downstairs. Not the person their parents kept insisting would come back if they ignored the truth long enough.

Lauren.

Their hands trembled against the edge of the desk, but this time it was not fear alone.

It was grief. Rage. Desperation. Relief.

Their grandfather was gone. The one person who might have shielded them, who might have made room for them, who might have told the rest of the family to shut up and sit down and listen.

So what were they waiting for now?

To be loved correctly by people who had never once tried?

To wake up one morning and find that pretending had somehow become survivable?

Lauren stood.

Smoothed the dress once with both palms.

Took one breath.

Then another.

Then they walked downstairs.

T HE CONVERSATION STOPPED BEFORE they had even reached the bottom step.

The silence spread fast and unnatural, like a light switching off in every room at once.

Their mother stood in the doorway between the kitchen and the living room, holding a casserole dish wrapped in foil. Their father had been talking to Uncle Ray, but now both men were staring. Aunt Linda's coffee cup hovered halfway to her mouth.

No one moved.

Lauren's heart pounded so loudly in their ears, they couldn't hear.

Still, when they spoke, their voice came out steadier than they expected.

"This is who I am."

The casserole dish slipped from their mother's hands and shattered across the hardwood.

Nobody bent to clean it up.

Their mother stared as if Lauren had walked into the room on fire. "What are you doing?"

"I'm Lauren." They forced themselves to look at her, then at their father. "I'm not who you keep saying I am. I'm not your son. I'm not your grandson. I'm me."

Their father's face darkened immediately. "Go upstairs."

"No."

"Go upstairs and change."

Lauren's entire body wanted to shake, but they held their ground. "I'm not changing."

Their mother made a broken little sound. "Today? You do this today?"

"Yes." Lauren's voice cracked. "Because Grandpa is gone, and he was the only person in this family who ever made me feel like I could breathe. And I can't keep doing this. I can't keep pretending for you. I can't keep disappearing just because it makes everyone else more comfortable."

Their father took one step forward. "Do not use my father to justify this."

"He would have understood."

"No." His voice turned sharp enough to slice the room in half. "He would not have wanted this spectacle in his house."

Spectacle.

The word landed hot and ugly.

Uncle Ray cleared his throat and took a small step back. Aunt Linda looked at the floor with the intense interest of someone desperate not to be involved.

Lauren's mother pressed a hand to her mouth. "I don't understand why you're doing this to us."

That almost made Lauren laugh.

To us.

As if their whole life had not been shaped around what everyone else could tolerate.

As if this had ever been about cruelty instead of survival.

Their father looked around the room, at the relatives standing there in horrified silence. "Everyone out."

Nobody argued. The house emptied in a rush of apologies, lowered eyes, awkward shoes on hardwood. Within a minute or two, the front door shut, and the silence that followed was somehow worse than the crowd had been.

Lauren stood alone in the living room with their parents and a puddle of casserole congealing slowly across the floor.

Their father's voice was cold when he spoke again. Too calm. Too precise.

"You have two choices."

Lauren knew, even before he finished, that nothing after those words would ever let them go back.

"You go upstairs, take that off, put on normal clothes, and we never speak of this again." He paused. "Or you leave."

For a second, Lauren thought they had heard wrong. "What?"

Their mother's eyes were red-rimmed and wet. "We love you," she said, and even in that moment Lauren heard the condition buried inside it. "But we can't encourage this. It isn't healthy. It isn't normal. You are confused and grieving and making everything worse."

"I'm not confused."

"Yes, you are."

"No." The word came out sharper than anything Lauren had said all day. "I'm finally telling the truth."

Their father folded his arms. "Then pack a bag."

Lauren stared at both of them, waiting.

Waiting for the correction. The softening. The moment where someone chose them over appearances and fear and whatever story they needed to tell themselves about what kind of family they were.

It never came.

Their mother cried.

Their father looked away.

That was the answer.

UPSTAIRS, LAUREN PACKED WITH shaking hands.

A duffel bag from the closet. A few changes of clothes. Toiletries. Makeup. Their phone charger. The sketchbook from under the bed. The handful of things that actually felt like they belonged to them and not to the life they had been assigned.

Their phone buzzed in the middle of shoving socks into a side pocket.

Lauren stared at the message until the screen blurred.

Then they hit call.

Willow answered on the first ring. "Hey. What happened?"

Lauren sat hard on the edge of the bed because their knees had suddenly stopped cooperating. "They kicked me out."

A beat of silence.

Then, very carefully, Willow said, "Tell me exactly what happened."

"I told them. I came downstairs and I told them who I

am and Dad said I either go change and pretend none of it happened or I leave." Their breath caught. "And I couldn't do it. I couldn't go back upstairs and put those clothes back on."

"No, you couldn't," Willow said instantly. No hesitation. No surprise. Just certainty. "Where are you right now?"

"My room."

"Okay. Pack what you need."

"I already am."

"Good. My mom said you can stay here as long as you want."

Lauren closed their eyes so hard it hurt. "Willow."

"No. Don't start. This is not a debate." Her voice gentled. "We're coming to get you. Me and my mom. Twenty minutes, max."

Lauren swallowed against the burn in their throat. "Thank you."

"That's what family is for," Willow said. Then, softer, "The real kind."

Lauren pressed the phone to their forehead for a second after the call ended.

The real kind.

Downstairs, a cabinet door slammed. Their father's voice carried faintly up the stairs, too low to make out.

Their mother started crying again.

Lauren zipped the duffel bag.

They did not look at the childhood photos on the dresser on the way out.

WILLOW'S MOM PULLED UP in a minivan twenty minutes later.

They walked out the front door in the pale blue dress with one duffel bag slung over their shoulder and their whole life reduced to what they could carry in two hands.

Their parents did not come outside.

They did not call after them.

They did not say goodbye.

The cold hit Lauren first. Then Willow.

Willow was out of the van before it had fully settled into park. She crossed the driveway fast and wrapped Lauren in a hug so fierce it almost knocked the breath out of them.

"You're okay. You're okay. I've got you."

Lauren did not feel okay.

They felt flayed open. Hollowed out. Furious. Terrified. Grief-stricken in ways that no longer had anything to do with the funeral.

But they let Willow hold them anyway.

Inside the van, Willow's mom turned around from the driver's seat and offered a sad, steady smile. "Hi, Lauren. I'm glad you're coming home with us."

Home.

The word hit harder than anything else had.

Lauren got into the van before they could start crying again.

WILLOW'S HOUSE SMELLED LIKE vanilla candles and laundry detergent and something simmering on the stove. Ordinary things. Safe things.

Willow carried the duffel bag upstairs while her mother fussed gently from the kitchen, asking if Lauren had eaten, if they wanted tea, if they needed towels. No interrogation. No staring. No strained silences built out of disapproval.

Just care.

In Willow's room, an air mattress had already been dragged from the hall closet and half-inflated.

"You can have the bed if you want," Willow said.

"No, it's okay."

"It really isn't."

Lauren almost laughed, which felt absurd under the circumstances. "The air mattress is fine."

Willow nodded. "You can do your makeup in here whenever you want. My mom said if you need space in the bathroom, just say so."

That nearly undid them all over again.

Their phone buzzed.

> **Jordan:** Willow told me. I'm so sorry.

> **Jordan:** Also, I am outside your parents' house thinking about throwing bricks. Proud of you, by the way. So, so proud.

Lauren stared at the screen until their vision blurred.

Then they sat down on the edge of Willow's bed in the pale blue dress and finally let themselves cry.

Not just for their grandfather.

Not just for the parents who had looked at them and chosen comfort over love.

For everything.

For the years spent hiding. For the terror of walking downstairs. For the ache of leaving with one bag and no goodbyes. For the sick, strange relief of no longer having to pretend.

Willow sat beside them without speaking and rested a hand between their shoulder blades.

Lauren cried until it hurt less.

Then a little more.

And somewhere beneath the grief and fear and exhaustion, something else began to take shape.

Not happiness. Not yet.

But relief.

A thin, trembling kind of freedom.

They were somewhere they did not have to hide.

Home was beginning to feel like a place that might actually want them back.

The First Door Opened

Sierra

BEFORE EVERYTHING CHANGED, SIERRA learned that being seen could feel almost as frightening as being ignored.

For years, her camera had been the place where everything made sense. Behind the lens, people revealed themselves. Moments slowed down. Chaos arranged itself into something honest and beautiful.

What she did not know yet was that someday someone would look back at her work and recognize not just a hobby, but a future. That one small *yes* could open a door she had not even known how to knock on.

Back then, she was a senior with a secondhand camera, a group chat full of chaos, and no real idea that her life was already beginning to take shape.

Senior Year

Ms. Trent caught Sierra after class on a Tuesday, and

Sierra's first thought was that she was in trouble.

"Can you stay for a minute?"

The classroom had mostly emptied by then. Chairs scraped, backpacks zipped, and the last few students drifted into the hallway in clumps of laughter and noise. Sierra lingered near the front of the room, trying not to look guilty even though she had no idea what she had supposedly done.

Ms. Trent gestured toward the desk beside hers. Sierra's latest photography assignment lay across it in a careful row of glossy prints.

The Coven, through Sierra's lens.

Calliope caught mid-laugh, mouth open and head thrown back like joy had physically grabbed hold of her.

Raven with her chin resting in one hand, expression dry and cutting even in stillness.

Jett looking down at something off-camera, smiling in a way so unguarded it felt almost private.

Sierra sat carefully, trying not to let her nerves show. "Is something wrong?"

Ms. Trent looked up, surprised. "Wrong? No. Quite the opposite."

She tapped the photo of Jett first. "These are remarkable."

Sierra glanced down, suddenly unsure where to put her

hands. "They're just my friends."

"That's exactly why they work." Ms. Trent leaned back in her chair. "Anyone can point a camera at a face. Not everyone can capture who a person is when they forget they're being watched."

Sierra felt warmth creep up the back of her neck.

"How long have you been doing this?"

"A couple years, I guess. Mostly for fun."

Ms. Trent smiled in a way that told Sierra she did not buy that for a second. "This is not just for fun, Sierra. This is craft. Instinct. Taste. You have a real eye."

No one outside the coven had ever said it like that before. Her family told her that she was creative. Teachers said nice things when assignments came in strong, but this felt different. Sharper. More serious.

"Have you thought about what you want to do after graduation?"

Sierra lifted one shoulder, trying for casual. "Photography, maybe. I don't know. My parents think it's more of a hobby."

"Well, your parents are not standing here looking at this work." Ms. Trent reached into a folder and pulled out a flyer. "The yearbook committee needs a new photographer. Our senior lead graduated early, and I'd love to have you on board."

Sierra took the flyer with both hands.

"And," Ms. Trent continued, "the Hartley Gallery is opening a new exhibit this weekend. It's small, but good. You should go. See what's being shown. Meet people. Start paying attention to the world you want to be part of."

Sierra stared at the flyer. The words Hartley Gallery looked suddenly enormous on the page.

"You really think I should?"

"I think if you're serious about this, you need to start acting like it." Ms. Trent's voice softened. "You are genuinely talented, Sierra. Don't let anyone convince you otherwise."

The words followed her all the way home.

H ER PHONE BUZZED JUST as she was dropping onto her bed that evening.

> **Calliope:** Movie night Friday. My place. Bring bad opinions and good snacks.

> **Raven:** I can do bad opinions. Good snacks remain to be seen.

> **Jett:** I will be there, gorgeous and underappreciated.

Sierra smiled and typed back.

> **Sierra:** I can't Friday. There's a photography exhibit I want to check out.

Three dots appeared immediately.

> **Calliope:** Fancy.

> **Jett:** We're obviously coming with you.

> **Sierra:** You do not have to come to a gallery just because I am going.

> **Raven:** This is not a discussion.

> **Calliope:** Also, I already decided what I'm wearing.

Sierra laughed out loud.

They never acted like the things that mattered to Sierra were small or silly or optional. If something lit her up, they crowded around it with real fuel.

Her phone buzzed again, but not from the group chat.

Sierra smiled before she could stop herself.

She stared at the message a second longer than necessary, then locked her phone and fell backward against the bed.

Salem, offended by the sudden movement, launched himself off her pillow with a sharp little chirp.

"Sorry. I'm having a life moment."

THE HARTLEY GALLERY WAS smaller than Sierra expected and somehow more beautiful because of it.

Exposed brick. High ceilings. Track lighting that made every photograph look almost holy. People drifted through the space in dark clothes and careful shoes, holding paper cups of wine and talking in low, serious voices that made everything feel important.

The coven arrived looking like they had coordinated for

a movie montage.

Calliope wore a vintage blazer over a black top and looked unbearably pleased with herself. Raven's eyeliner could have cut glass. Jett looked like he had stepped off the pages of a men's fashion magazine and somehow still seemed annoyed about it. Josh showed up in a charcoal sweater with one hand tucked into his pocket. When he smiled at Sierra from across the room, something in her chest gave its usual stupid little flip.

"You all look ridiculous," Sierra told them fondly.

"And yet," Calliope said, adjusting her lapel, "we are the best-dressed people here."

"That is objectively false," Raven said. "But I support the confidence."

Sierra drifted from piece to piece, letting the gallery swallow her whole. She studied lighting, shadow, framing, the quiet ways emotion lived inside a still image. Some photographs were gorgeous but empty. Others hit her like a punch, leaving something unsettled in her chest.

A photograph of a woman standing alone at a bus stop in the rain.

A portrait of two brothers shoulder to shoulder, both trying not to smile.

A grainy image of someone's grandmother at a kitchen table, flour on her hands and tired joy in her face.

Sierra stood in front of that one for a long time.

"First time at something like this?"

The voice came from beside her.

She looked up to find a man maybe in his late twenties or early thirties standing there with a camera bag slung over one shoulder and the sort of quiet confidence that suggested he knew exactly why he belonged in the room.

"Is it that obvious?" Sierra asked.

He smiled. "Only because you're looking at everything like you want to climb inside it."

That made her laugh. "Then yes. First time."

"Jonas."

He held out a hand. Sierra shook it.

"Sierra."

"You shoot?"

"A little." She instantly regretted how dismissive that sounded. "Mostly people. Portraits. Candid stuff."

Jonas nodded toward the far side of the room, where the coven and Josh had become a small island of dramatic hand gestures and conflicting opinions. "Those your people?"

Sierra smiled. "Yeah."

"They let you practice on them?"

"Constantly."

"That helps." He tilted his head. "Got anything on

you?"

Her heart kicked hard against her ribs. "My camera, yeah."

"Mind if I see?"

Sierra hesitated for only a second before pulling the camera from her bag. Her fingers felt suddenly too clumsy, too aware. She scrolled through recent shots and handed it over.

Jonas looked carefully. Not casually. Not politely. Carefully.

Jett laughing with his whole face.

Calliope and Raven in the middle of an argument that looked like it might end in homicide or a hug.

Josh glancing sideways at Sierra from across a cafeteria table.

Sunlight catching Raven in the school courtyard.

The longer Jonas looked, the quieter Sierra became.

Finally, he lowered the camera.

"You've got a good eye."

The words hit with almost physical force.

"Really?"

He handed the camera back. "Really. You're rough technically, which is normal, but you're seeing the right things. Most people starting out chase perfect lighting or cool angles and miss the actual heart of the image. You're watching for emotion."

Sierra curled her fingers around the camera strap. "That's what matters most to me."

"I can tell." Jonas glanced around the gallery, then back at her. "I had a mentor once. Gave me a chance when I had no business being anywhere near a professional set. Changed everything for me. So when I see someone with instinct, I try to pay attention."

Sierra was not sure she had blinked in the last ten seconds.

"I just had an intern quit. I've got a shoot this weekend. Nothing glamorous, but it's real work. Carrying equipment, setting up lighting, staying out of the way, paying attention. You interested?"

"Yes."

The answer flew out of her so fast that they both laughed.

Jonas pulled out his phone. "Good. Give me your number."

Sierra rattled it off while trying not to look like she was vibrating out of her own skin.

"One shoot. If you do well, maybe there are more. You flake on me, there definitely are not."

"That's fair."

"Very fair. Bring your camera, and wear shoes you can

stand in for hours."

Then, almost as an afterthought, he added, "You can do something with this, Sierra. If you want it badly enough."

After he walked away, Sierra stood completely still for several seconds.

Then Josh appeared at her shoulder and lightly bumped her arm. "Did that actually happen, or did I hallucinate the whole thing?"

"I honestly don't know."

That was enough to bring the others over in a rush.

"Who was that?" Calliope demanded.

"Jonas," Sierra said, still half stunned. "He's a photographer. He just offered me a job."

"A job?" Jett's voice shot up at least an octave.

Raven grabbed both of Sierra's shoulders. "I told you. I literally told you."

Josh was smiling at her in that soft, easy way that always made her feel steadier. "That's huge, Si."

Sierra looked around at all of them, the gallery lights warm overhead, her camera still clutched in one hand, and had the strange, disorienting feeling that maybe her life had just tilted.

Just a little, but enough.

DINNER THAT NIGHT STARTED out normal enough.

Her mother passed the potatoes. Tobias complained about homework. Thalia rolled her eyes so hard it was practically athletic. Their father asked if anyone had fed the dog next door while the neighbors were away, which somehow turned into a five-minute argument about responsibility and basic human decency.

Sierra waited until there was a lull.

"I got asked to join yearbook."

Her mom smiled. "That's nice, honey."

"And Ms. Trent thinks I should start taking photography more seriously." Sierra took a breath. "Like, professionally."

Her father glanced up from his plate. "Professionally how?"

"Editorial maybe. Portraits. Photojournalism. I don't know exactly yet." She tried to keep her voice steady. "But that's what I want to do after graduation."

The table quieted.

Not silent, exactly. Just careful.

"Photography," her mother said at last. "As a career."

"Yes."

Her parents exchanged a look that made Sierra's stomach sink before either of them even spoke.

"Honey," her mom began gently, "photography is a lovely passion. But passion and a stable income are not always the same thing."

"There are photographers with stable incomes," Sierra said.

"Of course," her father said. "But it's competitive. Hard to break into. Unpredictable."

"What about teaching?" her mom suggested. "Or graphic design? Something creative, but practical. You could always keep photography on the side."

"She doesn't want it on the side," Tobias said before Sierra could answer.

Their father looked at him. "We're just talking."

"No, you're doing that thing where you act supportive while telling her the thing she wants is unrealistic."

Sierra glanced at him, startled.

Thalia set down her fork. "He's right."

Their mother sighed. "We are not trying to crush anyone's dreams."

"Then maybe stop talking like success only counts if it comes with a pension and dental," Thalia said.

"Thalia," their dad warned.

But she kept going. "Sierra's been working at this for years. Her teacher sought her out. That matters. Not everyone gets that kind of recognition in high school."

"We're not saying it doesn't matter," their father said, more tired than angry. "We're saying she needs to be smart."

"She is being smart," Tobias said. "She's building experience. She's meeting people. She literally got invited to help on a professional shoot tonight."

That got both parents' attention.

"What?" her mother asked.

Sierra winced. She had not meant to bring up Jonas yet, mostly because the whole thing still felt too fragile and miraculous to expose to doubt.

"At the gallery. I met a photographer named Jonas. He looked at my work and asked if I wanted to assist on a shoot this weekend."

Her mother blinked. "A grown man invited you to work with him?"

"It's not like that."

"Honey, you don't know him."

"It's a professional opportunity," Sierra said, heat rising in her face now. "That's how networking works."

Their father rubbed a hand over his mouth. "You're still in high school."

"So what, I'm supposed to wait until I magically become older before taking anything seriously?"

"No one is saying that," her mom said.

"It kind of sounds like you are."

The words hung there.

Sierra stared down at her plate, throat tight. She had wanted to tell them about the yearbook committee and the gallery and Jonas because she was excited. Because part of her had hoped, stupidly maybe, that they would see what she saw. That they would hear it and understand this was real.

Instead, everything had narrowed into worry, suspicion, and practical concerns.

"I didn't want to fight," she said quietly. "I just wanted to tell you something good."

Silence settled over the table.

Her mother reached over and squeezed her hand. "We do love you. We worry because we love you."

Sierra nodded because that was easier than trying to explain the ache that had opened in her chest.

She excused herself before anyone could see the tears gathering in her eyes.

S ALEM WAS ALREADY WAITING on her bed when she got upstairs, curled into a black comma against her blanket like he had sensed the emotional collapse approaching and wanted front-row seating.

Sierra scooped him up and buried her face in his fur.

"You are the only uncomplicated being," she mumbled.

He purred, accepting this as his due.

Her phone buzzed almost immediately.

Calliope: Your parents did not get it, did they?

Sierra: How do you know every-thing?

Jett: Because adults hear art and immediately start acting like you announced a plan to join the circus.

Raven: For the record, I would support that too.

Calliope: Same. But also, you are going to kill it this weekend.

Jett: Literally already proud of you.

> **Raven:** Save this message for when you're famous and intolerable.

Sierra smiled in spite of herself.

Then another text came through.

> **Josh:** You're incredible. Don't let anybody make you doubt that.

That one landed differently.

She saved them all.

Every message. Every stupid joke. Every small piece of evidence that the people who loved her saw exactly what her family could not quite bring themselves to trust.

Sierra set the phone aside and lay back against the pillows, Salem sprawled across her chest like a warm, purring weight.

Her parents were worried.

Maybe they always would.

But the coven believed in her. Josh believed in her. Ms. Trent had seen something real in her work. Jonas had given her a chance.

The dream in her head no longer felt like a fantasy she had to protect in secret.

It felt like a road.

Unsteady. Unclear. Probably harder than she could imagine.

Still real.

She ran one hand down Salem's back and stared up at the ceiling.

She was doing this.

No matter who understood it.

No matter who didn't.

THE FIRST SHOOT WAS a disaster.

Not an obvious one. Nobody yelled. No equipment broke. Jonas didn't fire her on the spot, but Sierra fumbled a lens change so badly she missed the best candid of the whole session. She set up a reflector at the wrong angle twice. And when Jonas asked her to watch the model's expression for the right moment, she froze, too aware of her own inexperience to trust what she was seeing.

On the subway home, she sat with her bag in her lap and replayed every mistake until they felt enormous.

Her phone buzzed.

Jonas: Good first day. You'll get faster.

She stared at the message. It did not feel like a good first day.

The Chaos Coven lit up immediately after she posted a vague, self-pitying update.

> **Calliope:** Bad days are not the same as bad decisions.

> **Raven:** You showed up. That's the whole point.

> **Jett:** Also, Jonas literally asked you back. Stop spiraling.

Sierra almost laughed. Almost.

She was not sure yet whether showing up was enough. But the alternative—not showing up, not trying, retreating to the safe and familiar—felt worse.

So she would go back. She would be better. She would earn the chance she had been given, even if earning it meant surviving the days that made her question whether she deserved it at all.

Before everything changed, this was the first door that opened.

Building Something Beautiful

Lauren

BEFORE EVERYTHING CHANGED, LAUREN learned that survival and living were not the same thing.

For a long time, survival had been enough. It was a place to sleep, a locked bathroom door, and a few people who used the right name and meant it. Small mercies, carefully guarded.

Little by little, almost without noticing, survival began to shift into something else. Something brighter. Something with shape and ambition and room to breathe.

Back then, Lauren was seventeen, waking to the smell of pancakes in a house where their makeup bag no longer had to be hidden.

Senior Year

Lauren woke to sunlight spilling across Willow's bedroom floor and the smell of pancakes drifting upstairs.

For a few quiet seconds, they stayed where they were on the air mattress that had long since stopped feeling temporary. The room was warm. Willow was humming somewhere in the bathroom. A half-zipped makeup bag sat openly on the desk beside the ring light they had clipped there weeks ago.

No garbage bags. No hiding places. No frantic wiping away eyeliner before someone came in.

Just morning.

Just safety.

They still had moments sometimes, waking too fast and forgetting where they were, expecting the old house, the old fear, the constant tension of having to shrink themselves down before anyone could object to their existence. But those moments passed more quickly now.

Here, the air felt different.

"You awake?" Willow called around a toothbrush, poking her head out from the bathroom doorway.

Lauren pushed themselves upright and rubbed at their eyes. "Barely."

"Mom made pancakes. Also Jordan is coming over later because she needs makeup for some family thing and has decided twenty dollars makes her a patron of the arts."

Lauren laughed softly. "Twenty dollars is twenty dollars."

"That's the spirit."

Downstairs, Willow's mom stood at the stove flipping pancakes with the ease of someone who had been feeding people she loved her whole life.

She looked up when Lauren entered. "Morning, Lauren. Sleep okay?"

"Morning. Yeah." Lauren slid into a chair, still not quite used to answering to their name so casually, so naturally, in a kitchen full of morning light. "Thank you."

"There's coffee if you want it, and I'm making extra because the two of you eat like woodland creatures preparing for winter."

Willow dropped into the chair beside them with a snort. "That is so rude and so accurate."

Lauren smiled into their mug.

It was such a small thing, breakfast. Pancakes, coffee, and Willow stealing strawberries off the plate before they were meant to be served. But small things had started to matter differently now. They felt them more. Not because they were dramatic, but because they were steady. Repeating. Safe.

Safe had once felt like something temporary. A couch to crash on. A favor someone might eventually regret.

Here, it had started to feel like structure.

Like home.

AFTER BREAKFAST, LAUREN SPREAD their make-up across Willow's desk in a neat little explosion of brushes, palettes, tubes, and jars. Their phone was propped on a stack of books to film. The ring light cast a soft glow over the setup.

Willow flopped onto the bed behind them. "What are we doing today?"

"Trying a new eye look I saw online." Lauren adjusted the angle of the phone camera. "I thought I'd film it if it doesn't go horribly."

"For Instagram?"

"Yeah."

They tried to say it casually, but Willow had already sat up.

"I hit five hundred followers last week."

Willow stared at them. "Lauren."

Lauren laughed a little. "What?"

"That is huge."

"It's not huge."

"It is literally five hundred people choosing to look at your work on purpose."

When Willow put it like that, Lauren felt warmth bloom in their chest.

They opened Instagram and scrolled through the comments on their latest post.

@makeupbymaya: Your blending is INSANE!

@trans_and_glam: This is goals. Tutorial please??

@priya_does_makeup: Following. Your work is beautiful.

Willow leaned over their shoulder. "See? I'm not saying this to gas you up. People love what you do."

Lauren took a screenshot and added it to the folder they had started keeping months ago. Screenshots of nice comments. Messages. Small wins. Proof that this was real. Proof that they were not imagining the life they were trying to build.

Then they pressed record and began.

Their voice came more easily now. They explained what brush they were using, why they were blending one shade before layering another, how light changed the finish of shimmer, where to soften the line so the whole look stayed wearable instead of theatrical.

It felt natural in a way that still surprised them.

There had been a time not long ago when speaking aloud as themselves had felt nearly impossible.

Now they were filming tutorials.

Now they were teaching.

JORDAN ARRIVED AROUND TWO with her usual chaotic energy and a tote bag that looked heavy enough to contain a small animal.

"I need you to make me look like a person who did not spend half the night having an academic breakdown over the French Revolution."

Lauren gestured toward the chair. "That bad?"

Jordan dumped the bag onto the floor and collapsed into the seat. "I wrote ten pages that somehow managed to be both historically informed and emotionally unstable."

Willow, stretched across the bed, did not even look up from her phone. "That's your brand."

"Thank you for your support."

Lauren smiled and studied Jordan's face, already mapping it in their head. "What's the event?"

"My cousin's wedding. Apparently I'm expected to look presentable."

"I can work with presentable."

"As opposed to your usual vibe," Willow said sweetly, "which is exhausted menace."

Jordan pointed at her. "Do not speak to me while I am vulnerable."

Lauren laughed and reached for the primer.

As they worked, Jordan scrolled through her phone, then gasped. "Oh my God. You posted that tutorial already?"

"This morning."

"You are so talented it's genuinely irritating. I can barely manage eyeliner without looking haunted and you're out here making faces look expensive."

"It's just practice."

Jordan lowered the phone and looked at Lauren in the mirror. "No. It's not just practice. It's skill."

Willow nodded from the bed. "Exactly."

Jordan turned the screen around. "Also, your post already has fifty likes."

Lauren stared.

Fifty.

Comments were stacking up too. People asking what products they used. Whether the look would work on hooded eyes. If they took bookings.

"See?" Jordan said. "People are paying attention."

Lauren tried to focus on blending out Jordan's contour,

but something in their chest had started to flutter.

"You should start charging properly," Jordan added. "Not just the fake little friend price where you basically get paid in gratitude and stale chips."

"I don't know if I'm ready."

"You are."

Lauren gave her a look. "Very convincing."

"I'm serious. You did my makeup for homecoming and six people asked who did it. That girl in your history class asked about prom. You have followers. People are asking questions. This is not a hobby in the casual sense anymore."

Willow sat up again. "She's right. You keep acting like this is pretend, but it's not."

Lauren's hands paused.

The brush hovered over Jordan's cheek.

"What if people don't think I'm worth paying?"

Jordan's answer came instantly. "Then they're idiots."

Willow snorted.

Jordan shrugged. "What? It's true. They will pay because you're good. You don't have to be the most famous makeup artist in Brooklyn tomorrow. You just have to stop undervaluing yourself."

Lauren looked at their reflection in the mirror behind Jordan's shoulder. At the person standing there with a brush in one hand and a client in their chair and a small but growing audience online.

Client.

The word lodged itself somewhere new inside them.

J ORDAN LEFT TWENTY DOLLARS lighter and looking beautiful.

She spun once in the doorway before leaving. "If anyone at this wedding asks who did my makeup, I'm giving them your handle and charging referral fees."

"You absolutely are not."

"You can't stop me."

After the door shut, Lauren sat back down at the desk and opened Instagram again.

Five hundred thirty-two followers.

The tutorial from that morning had climbed again. Seventy-three likes. More comments. A direct message asking about prom makeup.

Their pulse picked up.

They took a screenshot and sent it to the group chat.

> **Lauren:** Someone wants to actually book me for prom makeup. What do I even charge?

Willow: Whatever your time and skill are worth.

Jordan: Minimum fifty.

Lauren: That feels illegal.

Jordan: It is called labor.

Willow: She's right.

Lauren read the message from the potential client three times before typing back.

@laurenluminary: I do have availability for prom makeup. My rate is $50 for a full face. Feel free to DM me if you want to book.

They hit send before they could overthink it.

Then immediately wanted to throw the phone across the room.

"This was a mistake," they announced.

"It was not," Willow said from the bed.

"I have made a terrible and arrogant choice."

"Lauren."

"I charged money."

"For a service," Willow said, like she was explaining gravity to a toddler. "This is not a crime."

Within an hour, three DMs came in.

Then a fourth.

Lauren stared at the screen in open disbelief.

"Willow."

"What?"

"I have three prom bookings."

Willow screamed so loudly her mother yelled up the stairs to ask whether someone was dying.

"No," Willow shouted back. "Lauren's becoming an entrepreneur."

THAT NIGHT, LAUREN LAY on the air mattress scrolling through their phone while the room around them softened into dark.

Five hundred forty-seven followers.

Four confirmed prom bookings.

A tutorial people were actually watching, saving, and asking questions about.

Six months earlier, they had been sitting in their parents' car with smeared eyeliner and a grief so sharp it had felt impossible to survive. Their whole life had fit into one duffel bag. Their future had been a blank wall.

Now they were not just surviving the days as they came.

They were making something.

A name. A little business. An identity.

Their phone buzzed again.

@makeupbymaya: Hey. I love your work. I run a small beauty page and would love to feature you if you'd be interested.

Lauren read the message once.

Then again.

Then a third time, because surely they had misunderstood something.

Featured.

Someone wanted to feature their work.

Their fingers stumbled a little as they typed back.

@laurenluminary: I'd be honored. Thank you so much.

The reply came fast.

@makeupbymaya: Amazing. I'll send the details tomorrow. Your blending technique is seriously goals.

Lauren made a sound so unhinged that Willow dropped her book.

"What happened?"

Lauren shoved the phone at her.

Willow read the message and let out a delighted gasp. "Oh my God."

Lauren had already screenshot it and sent it to the group

chat with a string of incoherent characters that translated roughly to holy shit holy shit holy shit.

A soft knock came at the door.

Willow's mom poked her head in. "Everything okay? I heard either excellent news or a very small exorcism."

Lauren laughed, breathless. "Good news."

"The kind that requires ice cream?"

"Maybe."

"Then it definitely requires ice cream."

LATER, THE THREE OF them sat around the kitchen table with bowls of chocolate chip ice cream sweating gently under the light.

Lauren told them about the bookings, the comments, the feature request, and the way each tiny thing felt unreal until the next one happened and made it harder to dismiss.

Willow's mom truly listened—actually listened—in a way that still made Lauren a little emotional when they let themselves think about it too long.

When Lauren finished, she smiled and said, "I'm proud of you."

The words were simple.

No dramatic speech. No big performance.

Just true.

Lauren looked down at their bowl because the sudden tightness in their throat felt dangerous. "Thank you. For letting me stay. For supporting this, and supporting me."

Willow's mom reached across the table and squeezed their hand. "You're family."

There it was again.

Family.

Not used as leverage. Not used to shame. Not used as something Lauren had to earn by disappearing.

Just given.

Plain and certain.

THAT NIGHT, BACK UPSTAIRS, Lauren opened Instagram one more time.

They updated their bio slowly, thinking about every word.

Makeup artist | Brooklyn | Bookings open | Building something beautiful

They stared at it a moment, thumb hovering over the screen.

Then they added one more line.

They/Them | Trans & Proud

Their heartbeat thudded hard enough to make their fingertips feel unsteady.

This was different from telling Willow and Jordan.

Different from letting safety hold the truth in private.

This was public. Visible. Unmistakable.

They hit save.

For one awful second, their whole body locked.

Then the first comment appeared.

@trans_and_glam: SO proud of you <3

@makeupbymaya: Yes!! Love this for you

@priya_does_makeup: Trans artists supporting trans artists <3

Lauren read each one slowly.

Then again.

Then took screenshots and saved them in the folder with all the others. They set the phone on their chest and stared up at the ceiling in the dark.

They were not just surviving anymore.

They were building a future out of brushes and light and courage. Love that made room instead of demands.

They were building something beautiful.

The Life She Chose

Sierra

BEFORE EVERYTHING CHANGED, SIERRA learned that sometimes one dream begins just as another is ending.

Those things don't cancel each other out. One doesn't make the other less real. But growing up has a cruel way of asking you to open one hand while the other is still full.

Back then, Sierra was still learning that happiness could shift shape without disappearing. That heartbreak could arrive gently. That building a future sometimes meant stepping toward one life while quietly grieving another.

She did not know yet how many things photography would give her. Only that the first time someone treated her talent like it belonged in the real world, her whole body sat up and paid attention.

Senior Year

The shoot with Jonas was chaos wrapped in adrenaline.

Sierra showed up at the address he had texted her, a converted warehouse in Red Hook with tall windows, peeling brick, and enough equipment inside to make her feel instantly underqualified. Light stands clustered near the walls. Backdrops hung in rolls from the far side of the studio. Cables snaked across the concrete floor in careful, dangerous lines.

Jonas was already there, adjusting a light. The precision of someone who'd done this enough times that his hands knew the way.

He spotted her, checked his watch, and nodded once. "You're early. Good."

Sierra tightened her grip on her camera bag. "I didn't want to be late."

"Excellent instinct. Help me with these lights while we wait for the models."

She stepped forward immediately. "What do you need?"

Jonas pointed to a stand near the wall. "Grab that. We're building a three-point setup."

Sierra hauled it over, trying not to look as nervous as she felt. "I know what that is in theory."

"In theory is a great place to start." Jonas took the stand from her, loosened a knob, and adjusted the height. "Key light here. Fill over there. Back light behind the subject if we want separation. The exact setup changes, but the logic stays the same. Light is storytelling. You decide what matters, then you shape the room around it."

Sierra absorbed every word.

For the next twenty minutes, he walked her through stands, modifiers, placement, angles, and why one tiny shift could change the entire mood of an image. Sierra listened like she was being handed access to some secret language she had always wanted to speak.

Then the models arrived, and everything sped up.

The next four hours passed in a blur of movement and instructions.

Hold this reflector.

Swap that lens.

Raise the backdrop.

Move left. No, your other left.

She ran on instinct, nerves, and the coffee Jonas shoved into her hand halfway through the second setup. She watched the way he talked to the models, how he adjusted his tone depending on who stood in front of the camera. The shy one got reassurance. The confident one got specificity. The awkward one got jokes until they loosened up.

It was not just about lighting.

It was about people.

That part made sense to Sierra immediately.

"See that?" Jonas said at one point, not taking his eye

from the viewfinder. "Her expression changed the second she stopped posing and started reacting. That's the shot. Anybody can photograph a face. The trick is getting the person."

Sierra followed his gaze and filed the moment away.

That was exactly it.

By the time the shoot wrapped, her feet hurt, her brain felt overclocked, and she had never been more awake in her life.

Jonas reviewed shots on the monitor while Sierra coiled cables and packed equipment with careful hands.

Finally, he looked over at her. "You did good."

She blinked. "Yeah?"

"You listened. Didn't panic. Didn't drop anything expensive. Asked smart questions." He turned back to the monitor. "You available next weekend?"

Sierra forgot to answer for half a second.

Then, "Yes. Absolutely."

Jonas nodded like that settled it. "Good. I've got an engagement shoot in Prospect Park. Bring your camera. I'll let you shoot second angle."

Her heart gave one huge, stunned leap. "Really?"

He smirked without looking up. "Don't make me regret it."

But he was smiling.

THE ENGAGEMENT SHOOT CHANGED something.

Sierra didn't realize it at the time. She was too busy adjusting her settings, finding angles, trying to prove she belonged behind the camera. The couple, Dani and Marcus, had been together for four years. They touched each other like it was second nature. No performance. Just the gravity of bodies that had learned each other.

Jonas positioned them near the boathouse while the light went gold. Sierra shot from the side, catching the moments between poses. Marcus tucking a strand of hair behind Dani's ear. Dani laughing at something he whispered. The way their hands found each other every time Jonas asked them to reset.

At one point Dani looked at Marcus and her whole face went soft. Not smiling, exactly. Just open. Like she had stopped performing for the camera entirely and was simply looking at the person she loved.

Sierra got the shot. She knew instantly that it was the best frame of the day.

Afterward, packing the gear into Jonas's car, she felt strange. Not sad. Not jealous. Something subtler and harder to name, like she'd been handed a photograph of a room she'd never been inside.

She knew what love looked like through a lens. She'd been documenting it for months now. The way people softened around the person who knew them best. The way a glance could carry more weight than a speech.

She'd had that with Josh. Hadn't she?

Yes, she had, but even with Josh, some part of her had been watching from a slight distance, composing the frame instead of standing inside it. She'd loved him. That was real. But she wasn't sure she'd ever looked at anyone the way Dani looked at Marcus, like the rest of the world had gone blurry and only one face stayed sharp.

Maybe she just hadn't met the right person yet.

Maybe the right person would make her stop composing and just be.

She shook the thought off and climbed into the passenger seat. Jonas handed her a coffee without comment, as if he could sense she'd gone somewhere private and was politely not following.

S IERRA BURST INTO CALLIOPE'S basement that night feeling like she was made entirely of momentum.

The coven was already assembled in their usual chaos. Blankets everywhere. Chips open. A movie paused on the television at what looked like a particularly bad decision on the part of a doomed blonde teenager.

"Jonas wants me to shoot second angle next weekend."

Calliope screamed first.

Jett followed with a slow clap so dramatic it crossed over into performance art. Raven got to her feet and pulled Sierra into a hug so fierce it nearly knocked the air from her lungs.

"I told you," Raven said against her shoulder. "I literally told you."

Josh stood a second later and wrapped his arms around her from the side, warm and solid and smiling into her hair.

"I'm so proud of you."

Sierra melted into him for a moment.

Safe. Celebrated. Wanted.

And still, somewhere under all of it, something restless flickered.

Not wrong.

Just unfinished.

THREE MONTHS LATER, SIERRA was spending more time with Jonas than almost anyone, except the coven.

Her weekends belonged to shoots. Weeknights disappeared into editing tutorials, portfolio curation, and practicing until her eyes blurred from screen glare. Her camera had become such a constant extension of her body that she sometimes reached for it when it was already in her hands.

It was working.

Not perfectly. Not magically.

Josh's life was moving too, just in a different direction.

He was buried in applications, scholarship essays, and SAT prep books that looked dense enough to be used as weapons. Boston University had become less of a hope and more of a future fact waiting to happen.

So when he told her the news, it did not blindside her.

It still hurt.

They were sitting in his car outside her house after a movie, parked beneath a streetlamp that made everything look softer than it really was.

Josh kept both hands on the steering wheel for a second too long before speaking.

"I got in."

Sierra looked at him. "Boston?"

He nodded.

Something in his face was bright with pride and heavy with something else. "Full ride."

Her chest squeezed. "Josh, that's amazing."

"It is." He gave a small laugh that did not quite reach his eyes. "It's exactly what I wanted."

Sierra waited.

He turned toward her, shoulders shifting like he was bracing for impact. "We should talk."

There it was.

She had known.

She had still hoped maybe she was wrong.

"Yeah," she said quietly. "We should."

Josh looked down at his hands. "I love you."

He said it simply, without drama, and that somehow made it hit harder.

Sierra swallowed. "I love you too."

"I'm going to Boston. You're building something here." He glanced back at her. "And I don't think either of us should pretend that long distance is a romantic gesture if what it really means is both of us hanging on until it turns ugly."

Tears pressed hot behind Sierra's eyes, but she blinked them back long enough to really hear him.

He was not trying to escape her.

He was trying to be honest with her.

"We'd spend all our time missing each other. You'd be on shoots. I'd be drowning in coursework. We'd turn something good into something exhausting."

The tears came anyway.

Sierra laughed shakily and wiped at them. "You really had to be mature about this, huh?"

Josh smiled then, small and sad. "I thought about being a coward. It seemed less fair."

She looked at him and felt the ache of how much she cared for him. How grateful she was that he had been her first real love. How strange it was that heartbreak could hurt and still feel undeniably right.

"So what are we saying?" she asked.

Josh reached over and took her hand. "That this mattered. That it still matters. That ending it now doesn't make it less real."

Sierra squeezed his fingers. "You're one of the best things that ever happened to me."

His mouth twitched. "Same."

They sat there a long time after that, hands linked between them, both crying a little and laughing at themselves for crying. The whole thing felt almost unbearably tender. Like they were not destroying something, just setting it down carefully before distance and time could ruin it for them.

When Sierra finally climbed out of the car and stood on the sidewalk looking back at him, she felt wrecked.

Not broken.

Just sad.

And okay.

Both at once.

THE COVEN MOBILIZED WITHIN minutes.

Calliope: Emergency movie night. My place. Now.

Raven: Bringing ice cream and emotional support.

Jett: On my way. Josh is a good guy, but still objectively foolish.

Sierra: It was mutual. Also, he is not foolish.

Calliope: Doesn't mean it doesn't suck. Get over here.

Sierra showed up to find blankets piled on the floor, her favorite deeply terrible horror movie queued up, and enough snacks to sustain a minor apocalypse.

They did not make her talk right away.

They always seemed to know when support meant conversation and when it just meant presence.

So Sierra curled into the corner of the couch with Raven's blanket over her legs, Calliope's socked feet shoved half into her lap, and Jett sprawled dramatically across the beanbag like a Victorian orphan with good hair.

About halfway through the movie, during a scene involving a basement no sane person would ever walk into, Calliope broke the silence.

"You know what this means, though."

Sierra did not look away from the screen. "I hate the tone of your voice already."

"You are officially free to notice when other people are attractive."

Sierra whipped a pillow at her.

Calliope caught it with annoying ease. "Too soon?"

"By a lot."

Raven, without lifting her eyes from the bowl of popcorn in her lap, said, "To be fair, you have been noticing."

Sierra stared at her. "Excuse me?"

Raven shrugged. "The girl in your art class."

Calliope gasped theatrically. "Yes. Starlight girl."

"There is no starlight girl."

"There is absolutely a starlight girl," Jett said. "You talked about her for twenty minutes after the homecoming game. How her hair caught the stadium lights. How she smiled at you like she knew something you didn't."

Sierra's stomach dropped because she remembered that night with embarrassing clarity. The girl had been standing near the bleachers in a denim jacket, laughing with friends, and Sierra had felt something tilt inside her chest so hard she'd had to look away.

She'd never learned her name.

"That doesn't mean anything," Sierra said, but even she could hear how thin it sounded.

Jett gave her a look that was gentle and completely undeceived. "Also, for the record, you notice people. Like, really notice them. Not just Josh. You always have."

Calliope put a hand to her chest. "I prefer to inspire both."

Sierra buried her face in the blanket. "I am never speaking again."

Calliope scooted closer until their shoulders bumped. Her voice softened when she spoke next. "You don't have to know exactly what you are yet."

Sierra looked up.

Raven nodded once. "But you do have to stop acting like noticing girls is some weird side effect instead of part of the truth."

Jett offered her the popcorn bowl. "You can be in the middle for as long as you need."

Her shoulders dropped.

Not into certainty. Not yet.

But into permission.

LATER, AFTER CALLIOPE HAD fallen half asleep with her mouth open and Jett had become one with the beanbag, Sierra lay awake under a pile of mismatched blankets and let herself sit with the truth she had been circling for months.

She had loved Josh.

That was real.

She also noticed girls.

That was real, too.

Not in a theoretical way. Not in a maybe if she thought about it long enough way. In a body-deep, heart-quickening, undeniable way.

She still did not have the exact word for herself.

But she was getting closer.

Closer felt important.

Closer felt like movement.

Two weeks later, Jonas called and told her to meet him at his Bushwick studio.

An actual studio this time, not borrowed space. Brick walls, high shelves full of equipment, framed prints leaning against one side of the room, and the distinct smell of coffee, dust, and old camera bags.

"Sit," he said, gesturing toward a stool.

Sierra sat.

Her knee started bouncing before she could stop it.

Jonas leaned against his desk and folded his arms. "You've been shadowing me for four months."

The words made her stomach drop a little, because four months sounded like the beginning of a conversation that could go in any direction.

"You learn fast. You listen. You take criticism without getting weird about it. Your eye is getting better every week."

Sierra tried not to blink too hard.

"I want to make this more official."

Her whole body went still.

"You shoot second angle on my gigs. I pay you a percentage. You keep building your portfolio, and I teach you what I know." He shrugged one shoulder. "That arrangement work for you?"

Sierra's throat went tight so quickly she almost could not answer. "Yes."

Jonas smiled a little. "Good."

"Seriously. Yes. More than yes. This is..." She let out a breath that felt half laugh, half disbelief. "This is everything."

"Don't romanticize me too much. This industry will chew people up if they let it. But if you keep showing up, keep learning, and stop apologizing every time someone says you're talented, you've got a real shot."

Sierra swallowed hard and nodded. "I will."

"I know." He handed her a printed call sheet from the desk. "First official job is Saturday. Don't be late."

She laughed then, bright and startled and so relieved it bordered on dizzy.

S HE TEXTED THE COVEN before she even made it to the subway.

Sierra: Jonas just made it official. He hired me. I'm really doing this.

Jett: HELL YES

Calliope: We knew you when etc. etc. Please remember us when you're rich and insufferable.

Raven: Seriously proud of you.

Sierra stared down at the messages while people moved around her on the platform, everyone rushing toward their own lives, their own evenings, their own futures.

Hers did not feel abstract anymore.

That night, sitting cross-legged on her bed with Salem trying to sit directly on her phone, Sierra opened Instagram and updated her bio.

Photographer | NYC | Available for bookings

She looked at the words for a long time after she had hit save.

Simple. Maybe even a little ridiculous.

But real.

Not a dream, she whispered to herself in the dark. Not a hobby people patted her on the head about. Not a some-day life, waiting for permission.

A beginning.

She scratched behind Salem's ears and smiled when he started purring hard enough to vibrate.

"I'm doing this, little buddy."

He blinked at her, deeply unsurprised.

Sierra set the phone down beside her and leaned back against the wall, heart still humming with the strange, fragile thrill of becoming.

Josh was gone now, or almost.

The future was still uncertain.

Her heart was still full of questions she could not yet name.

But photography was no longer one of them.

Before everything changed, this was the life she had chosen.

The Future They Said Yes To

Lauren

BEFORE EVERYTHING CHANGED, LAUREN learned that sometimes the life you were meant for arrived disguised as logistics.

A contract. A booking. A train ride. A room for rent. A chance that looked too fragile to trust until it kept returning, again and again, asking the same question in different forms.

Are you going to stay where it's safe, or are you going to become who you are meant to be?

Back then, Lauren was finishing high school with one hand on a makeup brush and the other on a future that still felt a little too bright to look at directly.

Senior Year

Lauren had fifteen minutes between finishing their calculus final and meeting a client for graduation makeup.

Fifteen.

Which meant no time to spiral, no time to overthink whether they had bombed the exam, and definitely no time to sit in the weird emotional whiplash of calculating derivatives one minute and contouring somebody's cheekbones the next.

They bolted from the testing room with their backpack half-zipped and their heart still thudding from the exam, then jogged across the parking lot toward Willow's car.

Willow was already in the driver's seat with Lauren's makeup kit buckled into the passenger side like a very glamorous child.

Lauren yanked the door open and climbed in. "Drive."

Willow pulled out of the lot immediately. "How'd it go?"

Lauren dropped their head back against the seat. "I either passed with surprising dignity or failed so hard I altered the space-time continuum. No middle ground."

Willow snorted. "Sounds like calculus."

Lauren pulled out their phone and checked Instagram out of habit. Three new DM requests. Two comment notifications. One booking inquiry from someone with a profile picture that looked aggressively rich.

They opened the note with the client's address.

"You're doing graduation makeup during finals week," Willow said. "That is either impressive or deeply concerning."

"I'm broke. There's a difference."

"You are not broke. You are, like, medium successful."

Lauren gave her a look. "Medium successful does not pay Manhattan rent."

Willow glanced over. "Ah. So we're worrying about the future before noon. Good. Love that for us."

Lauren looked down at their hands. "I just need to save. I know college probably isn't happening right away, but if I'm going to keep doing this seriously, I need money. First month's rent somewhere. Supplies. MetroCards. Life."

Willow's expression softened. "You're allowed to want more than survival, you know."

Lauren stared out the window for a second, watching the city slip by in flashes of traffic lights, bodegas, brick, and chain-link fences.

And that was it, wasn't it?

They wanted more now.

Which was equal parts thrilling and terrifying.

THE CLIENT'S HOUSE SAT on a tree-lined street in one of those neighborhoods that looked like everyone inside the homes had matching towels and no credit card debt.

At first, places like this had made Lauren feel instantly out of place. Too aware of their clothes, their bag, the way their accent flattened certain vowels when they were nervous. But over the last several months, that feeling had started to loosen. Work helped. Skill helped. Having a reason to be there helped most of all.

They were not there to impress anyone.

They were there because someone had hired them.

That mattered.

The girl who opened the door introduced herself as Chloe and looked exactly like someone who had never once had to wonder whether her parents would still love her after the truth came out.

Lauren hated that they thought that. Then hated themselves a little for thinking it. Then shoved the entire spiral aside because Chloe was already smiling nervously and saying, "I'm so glad you're here."

Inside, the house smelled faintly of lemon polish and expensive candles. Graduation balloons clustered in one corner of the dining room. Somewhere in the kitchen, somebody was yelling about missing heels.

Chloe led Lauren upstairs to a bedroom flooded with natural light.

"I've been following you on Instagram for months," she

said while Lauren set up brushes and palettes on the vanity. "Your work is amazing. When my mom said I could hire someone, you were literally the first person I thought of."

The warmth hit Lauren's chest so suddenly it almost embarrassed them. "Thank you. That really means a lot."

Chloe sat down and tucked her hair behind her ears. "I want something natural but glowy. Like, I still want to look like me, just better than me."

Lauren smiled. "That's my whole thing, actually."

And it was.

That realization came to them more clearly each time they worked on someone new. They were not trying to turn people into strangers. They were trying to bring them into sharper focus. To make them look in the mirror and recognize themselves with a little more tenderness than before.

Maybe that was part of why makeup mattered so much to them.

It was never really about hiding.

It was about revealing.

They worked in easy quiet for a while, trading small comments about school, finals, the surreal feeling of being almost done with high school while not yet belonging to whatever came next.

Lauren's hands moved with growing confidence.

Primer. Foundation. Concealer. Cream blush. A whisper of shimmer across the lids. A soft highlight placed exactly where it would catch the afternoon light.

They knew what they were doing now.

Not perfectly. Not arrogantly. But truly.

About halfway through, Chloe's voice turned more careful.

"Can I ask you something?"

Lauren looked up from blending her bronzer. "Sure."

"My cousin is questioning some stuff. Gender stuff, I think." Chloe twisted her fingers together in her lap. "And I just... I don't want to be the kind of person who says the wrong thing and makes it worse. Your Instagram says you're trans, so I figured maybe you'd know."

Lauren paused for only a second.

Then they smiled, small and real. "Honestly? The best thing you can do is listen."

"That's it?"

"That's most of it." Lauren softened the line beneath Chloe's eye. "Don't try to solve it for them. Don't rush them. Let them figure it out in their own time, and if they tell you a name or pronouns they want to try, use them. Even if it changes later."

Chloe watched them in the mirror. "That sounds kind of simple."

Lauren met her eyes in the reflection. "It is simple. People just make it harder than it needs to be."

Chloe nodded slowly. "Being seen matters that much?"

Lauren set down the brush for a second. "It matters more than most people realize."

The room went quiet after that, but not awkwardly. Just thoughtful.

When Lauren finished, Chloe stared at herself in the mirror, and her eyes went wide.

"Oh my God."

Lauren froze for half a second. "Bad oh my God?"

"No." Chloe laughed, already reaching for a tissue. "No, I look like myself. But like the version of myself I actually wanted people to see today."

Something in Lauren's chest went soft.

"You already looked like yourself," they said gently. "I just helped bring it out a little."

When Chloe paid them, she handed over sixty dollars instead of the agreed fifty.

Lauren blinked. "This is too much."

"It's a tip."

"You don't have to tip me that much."

Chloe looked almost offended. "You're talented. Charge what you're worth."

The words stuck.

That was the second time in a week someone had said that.

Maybe, slowly, they were beginning to believe it.

B Y THE TIME LAUREN got back to Willow's house, their booking calendar looked like it was trying to stage a hostile takeover.

Four graduation makeup appointments that week.

Two prom clients the following weekend.

One girl who wanted headshots done with "clean girl glam" and had typed the phrase exactly like that.

Lauren sat cross-legged on the floor beside Willow's bed, updating times and addresses and product notes while Willow worked on some English assignment nearby and made occasional judgmental noises at her laptop.

Lauren checked Instagram again.

1,847 followers.

Still not massive. Still not influencer-level or anything close.

But more than enough to feel real.

They were halfway through editing photos for a tutorial when a new DM notification appeared from an account they did not recognize.

@GlamSquadNYC: Hey. We're a makeup collective in Manhattan. We saw your work and we're really impressed. We're currently looking for artists to join our team. Would you be interested in chatting?

Lauren read it once.

Then again.

Then a third time, because surely their brain was filling in words that were not actually there.

Manhattan.

A makeup collective.

A team.

An actual professional opportunity.

"Willow," they said carefully, in the tone of someone trying not to scream and failing.

Willow looked up. "What happened?"

Lauren turned the phone toward her. "Tell me if this is legit or if I'm being catfished by capitalism."

Willow snatched the phone and immediately reached for her own. "Hold on."

For the next thirty seconds, Lauren watched her type at alarming speed while their own pulse climbed into genuinely rude territory.

Then Willow looked up with huge eyes.

"It's real."

Lauren just stared.

Willow shoved her own phone toward them. "It's absolutely real. They do event makeup, editorial work, fashion stuff. Lauren, this is huge."

Their fingers had started shaking.

Very carefully, Lauren typed back.

@laurenluminary: I'm definitely interested. Thank you so much. When would you want to talk?

The response came within minutes.

@GlamSquadNYC: How about a video call this Saturday at 2?

Lauren swallowed hard and typed yes before fear could get in the way.

Then they set the phone down on the desk like it might explode.

Willow waited.

Lauren inhaled once.

Then screamed into a pillow.

Willow fell over laughing. "What did they say?"

"They want a video call on Saturday."

"Oh my God." Willow launched herself onto the air mattress in celebration, nearly knocking over a ring light. "You're doing this. You're actually doing this."

Lauren sat down more slowly. "I'm not doing anything yet. They just want to talk."

"People do not schedule professional calls for fun."

Lauren pressed both hands over their face. "What if I'm not ready?"

Willow's voice softened. "You've been ready for a while. You just still act like the world hasn't noticed."

Lauren felt that one land.

T HEY DID NOT SLEEP much that night.

Every time they started drifting off, a new thought shoved its way in.

Manhattan.

A real team.

Contract work.

Pay per job.

Maybe enough momentum to build an actual life.

But all of that came tangled with the other truth.

Leaving Willow's house.

Leaving the first place that had ever felt safe.

Leaving the people who had stitched them back together after everything else split apart.

They rolled onto their side and stared at the faint glow of Willow's fairy lights across the room.

Scary and exciting were starting to feel alarmingly similar.

THE VIDEO CALL HAPPENED in Willow's bedroom two days later.

Willow and Jordan insisted on being present for "emotional support and emergency homicide if needed," though they stayed just out of frame once the call began.

The woman on screen introduced herself as Tasha. She had flawless makeup, a sharp white blouse, and a composure Lauren associated with people who had never once doubted their right to take up space.

Tasha's smile was warm. "So, Lauren, tell me about yourself."

Lauren took a breath and sat up straighter.

"I'm eighteen and about to graduate. I've been doing makeup for about two years now. I started by teaching myself through YouTube and practicing on friends, then started building a client base through Instagram." They clasped their hands together in their lap to keep from visibly fidgeting. "I mostly do natural glam and editorial-inspired looks, but I'm flexible."

Tasha nodded. "And you want to do this professionally?"

More than anything, Lauren thought.

Out loud, they said, "Yes. I really do. Makeup is how I express myself, but also how I help other people feel seen. I love the technical side, but I also love the connection. Making someone feel comfortable in their own face matters to me."

Tasha smiled a little wider at that.

"I looked through your page. Your technique is strong. Your color sense is great. But what stood out most to me was how people respond to you. Your clients look comfortable. That matters more than people think."

Lauren nodded, not trusting themselves to interrupt.

"We're looking for artists who can handle events, shoots, and client-facing work under pressure. We'd start you on contract jobs. You'd get training with the team, and if things go well, there could be more opportunities down the line." Tasha tilted her head. "The only catch is that you'd need to be in Manhattan regularly. Is that realistic for you?"

Lauren's heart kicked hard.

No was the practical answer.

Maybe not yet was the careful answer.

But something in them had spent too long living as if practicality and fear were the same thing.

"I'll make it work," they said.

And they meant it.

Tasha smiled. "Good. I'll send over a contract for you to review. Take your time. Ask questions. If you're still interested after that, we'll set up an in-person meeting."

When the call ended, Lauren just sat there, staring at the black screen.

Jordan broke the silence. "That sounded good, right?"

Willow was already grinning. "That sounded very good."

Lauren laughed once, shaky and disbelieving. "She's basically offering me a job."

"She is offering you a job," Willow corrected.

"In Manhattan."

"In Manhattan," Jordan echoed, like she was announcing the opening act of Lauren's future.

Then reality came crashing back in.

"I don't have a place to live there," Lauren said. "I barely have enough saved to keep pretending I'm financially stable. I can't."

"One problem at a time," Jordan said.

Willow nodded. "First you figure out whether you want this. Then we figure out the logistics."

Lauren looked between them. "What if I'm not ready?"

"You are," Willow said immediately.

This time, Lauren did not argue.

THE DOUBT ARRIVED AT three in the morning, the way it always did.

Lauren lay awake scrolling through GlamSquad's Instagram. Every artist on their roster looked polished, certain, practiced in a way Lauren had never felt. Their portfolios gleamed with editorial credits and fashion week tags, and client lists that read like a who's who of New York beauty.

And then there was Lauren. Self-taught. No formal training. A portfolio built from bedroom tutorials and prom clients and exactly one professional feature on a beauty page with twelve thousand followers.

What if Tasha had made a mistake?

What if this was the moment where wanting something too badly finally caught up with them?

They closed Instagram and opened the notes app instead. Made a list:

Things I know how to do.

The list grew longer than they had expected. Color theory. Skin matching across undertones. Contouring for editorial versus natural versus bridal. Speed. Patience. Making nervous people feel comfortable in a chair.

They stared at the list until their breathing slowed.

Then they added one more line at the bottom:

Things I can learn.

That list was longer. But it didn't scare them the way it once would have.

THE CONTRACT ARRIVED THAT night.

Lauren read it twice on their phone, once more on Willow's laptop, then screenshot every section that confused them and sent them in a rapid-fire burst to Willow's mother, who worked as a paralegal and therefore possessed what Lauren considered borderline supernatural powers.

To Lauren's immense relief, she looked it over without hesitation.

"It's legitimate," she said later from the kitchen doorway while drying her hands on a dish towel. "Standard contract language. The pay is fair. Nothing here worries me."

Lauren looked down at the signature line.

This was it.

Not the biggest decision of their life, maybe. They had already made that one in a blue dress standing in a room full of casseroles and silence.

But it was close.

This was the next version of the same choice.

Stay small.

Or leap.

They thought about their parents.

About grief.

About Willow's mother saying, *welcome home.*

About every terrifying decision since then that had cracked open into something better than fear had promised.

Then they signed.

T HE FINAL WEEKS OF school passed in a blur of exams, appointments, cap-and-gown pickups, and exhaustion so constant it started to feel decorative.

Lauren did graduation makeup in strangers' bedrooms and prom makeup in over-air-conditioned suburban houses and one headshot session in a studio apartment so tiny they had to set their brushes on top of a microwave.

They were tired all the time.

They were also more alive than they had ever been.

One job stayed with them longer than the others.

A bride named Elena. Tiny apartment in Flatbush, barely room for the makeup chair and the ring light. Elena's hands trembled the entire time Lauren worked on her—not from nerves about the wedding, she said, but from disbelief that it was actually happening.

"I spent so long thinking I didn't get to have this," Elena said quietly, watching Lauren blend shadow across her lids. "A wedding. A person who chose me. The whole thing."

Lauren's brush paused for just a moment. "I know that feeling."

Elena met their eyes in the mirror. "Yeah. I thought you might."

When Lauren finished, Elena's wife—a tall woman with close-cropped hair and steady hands—came in to see her. She stopped in the doorway. Didn't say anything at first. Just looked at Elena like she was seeing her for the first time and the thousandth time simultaneously.

Elena laughed, teary. "Don't. You'll ruin my makeup."

"I won't touch your face," her wife said. "But you need to know you're the most beautiful person I've ever seen."

Lauren stepped back and pretended to organize their brushes. Gave them the moment. But something behind their ribs pulled tight—not grief, not envy, just a recognition so sharp it almost had a sound.

They wanted that.

Not the wedding. Not the ceremony, or the dress, or the flowers. The look. The way someone could see you across a room and go still because you were the thing that made everything else make sense.

Nobody had ever looked at Lauren like that.

They'd been seen—by Willow, by Jordan, by strangers online who loved their work. Seen as talented, as brave, as someone worth rooting for. That mattered. It mattered enormously.

But it wasn't the same thing.

On the subway home, Lauren stared at their reflection in the dark window and wondered what it would feel like. To be the person someone crossed a room for. To be chosen not for what they could do, but simply for who they were.

The train rocked, and the reflection wavered, and Lauren tucked the thought away where it wouldn't interfere with the work still ahead.

GRADUATION ITSELF HAPPENED ON a Thursday. Lauren crossed the stage in cap and gown, accepted their diploma, and kept walking.

They did not let themselves scan the crowd for people who were not there.

They had sent a card two months earlier. An actual

physical card, addressed to their old name, forwarded by a neighbor who still had their number. Inside, their mother's handwriting: We hope you're doing well. No signature from their father. Lauren had stared at it for a long time, then tucked it into the back of a drawer where it could exist without requiring a decision.

They did not think about what it would have felt like to hear their parents cheering.

Instead, they found Willow's family afterward in a blur of hugs, flowers, and Jordan shouting their name loud enough to alarm nearby grandparents.

Willow's mom pulled Lauren aside once the crowd thinned a little.

"I'm so proud of you," she said simply.

Lauren's throat tightened on instinct. "Thank you."

"No," she said, cupping Lauren's elbow gently. "I mean it. I am so proud of the life you're building."

That nearly undid them.

Lauren swallowed hard. "I can never thank you enough for everything you've done for me."

"You're family." She smiled, steady and warm. "Which brings me to the Manhattan issue."

Lauren blinked. "The what?"

"The living situation." Willow's mom shifted the bouquet she was holding. "I talked to my aunt. She lives in

Brooklyn and has a spare room. Her husband died a few years ago and she's been lonely. She said if you want the room, it's yours for as long as you need."

For a second, Lauren could not speak at all.

The words hit too hard and too fast.

A room.

A place.

A bridge into the next version of their life.

Tears spilled before they could stop them.

Willow's mom pulled them into a hug without making a fuss about it, and Lauren held on.

THAT NIGHT, BACK IN Willow's room, Lauren opened Instagram one more time.

They updated their bio carefully.

@laurenluminary Makeup Artist | Brooklyn | Contract work with @GlamSquadNYC | Building dreams one face at a time | They/Them | Trans & Proud

They stared at it for a long time after hitting save.

Then the comments started rolling in.

@makeupbyChloe: SO proud of you!!!

@trans_and_glam: You're going to kill it in Manhattan

@priya_does_makeup: Congrats on everything!

Lauren read every one and let themselves believe it, just for a moment.

They were not just surviving anymore.

They were not even just building.

They were moving.

Forward.

Into something bigger.

Into a life that had once felt impossible to imagine.

And the future, finally, did not look like something they had to endure.

It looked like somewhere they were allowed to go.

The Road Ahead

Sierra

Senior Year

Graduation day smelled of sunscreen and freshly cut grass.

Sierra sat in a folding chair on the football field, cap tilted just enough to irritate her mother later, robe sticking to the backs of her knees. The principal's voice floated across the humid air in slow, ceremonial waves, talking about futures and potential and doors opening. The words slid past her without sticking.

Instead, she watched Calliope two rows ahead, who was attempting to fold her program into increasingly elaborate origami shapes. Raven sat across the aisle, pretending not to notice, but clearly timing how long it would take before Calliope got caught. Jett had his phone hidden in his sleeve, thumbs moving with surgical precision.

Typical.

She smiled despite herself.

When her name was called, she stood, crossed the stage, shook a hand she would never remember, and accepted a diploma that felt lighter than she expected. Applause washed over her. Somewhere in the stands her family was cheering, probably taking too many photos.

But her eyes found the coven first.

Calliope was on her feet, screaming as if Sierra had just won an Olympic medal. Raven whistled sharply, fingers in her mouth. Jett had somehow smuggled in a small air horn, which earned him a horrified look from a teacher two rows over.

Sierra laughed out loud as she stepped off the stage.

That was the moment she would remember. Not the handshake. Not the speech. Just the sound of her people making it impossible to feel small.

AFTERWARD, THE FIELD DISSOLVED into clusters of families and photo sessions. Sierra endured the required lineup: solo pictures, pictures with her parents, pictures with Tobias and Thalia, pictures where everyone was instructed to "look natural," which always meant the exact opposite.

Her cheeks hurt from smiling.

Then Calliope grabbed her wrist.

"Coven photos. Non-negotiable."

"My mom..."

"Can survive without you for five minutes. Move."

Sierra let herself be dragged across the grass to where Raven and Jett were waiting. They didn't pose so much as collapse into each other — arms around shoulders, caps crooked, grinning like conspirators.

Someone's dad volunteered to take the picture.

"Say something iconic," he suggested.

Calliope didn't hesitate. "Say we made it."

"WE MADE IT!"

The shout came out ragged and loud, and completely sincere.

The camera flashed.

Sierra knew instantly it would be one of her favorite photos of all time.

LATER, WHEN THE CROWD thinned, and the sun dipped lower, the four of them sank onto the grass in a loose circle, robes pooled around them.

No parents. No teachers. No expectations.

Just them.

"So," Jett said finally, pulling at a loose thread on his sleeve. "What happens now?"

Calliope answered first. "Community college. Staying local. Journalism program." She shrugged. "Baby steps."

"Same school," Raven added. "Different major. Psychology."

Jett nodded. "Gap year. Maybe two. I need to figure out who I am when I'm not just surviving high school."

They looked at Sierra.

She picked at a blade of grass, twisting it between her fingers. "Jonas offered me regular work. Real work. Second shooting, assisting, maybe more." She swallowed. "No college. At least not right now."

"Terrifying," Raven said.

"Extremely," Sierra agreed. "But it feels right. Like if I don't try this now, I'll regret it forever."

Calliope studied her for a moment, then smiled. "You've never looked more sure of anything."

Silence settled again, soft this time.

"We're all doing different things," Jett said quietly.

"Yeah," Raven added. "Different directions."

Calliope pressed her palm flat on the grass between them. "Then we make a pact."

Sierra blinked. "A pact?"

"No matter what happens," Calliope said, eyes suddenly serious, "no matter where we end up, we don't lose each other. The Coven doesn't expire just because high school did."

One by one, they stacked their hands on top of hers.

"The coven is forever," Jett said.

"Forever," Raven echoed.

Sierra placed her hand last, feeling the warmth of all of them beneath it. For a moment, the future didn't feel like a cliff. It felt like a wide open road — scary, yes, but not lonely.

She wished she had her camera. But some moments weren't meant to be captured. They were meant to be carried.

Around them, the field was emptying. Couples drifted toward the parking lot hand in hand. Someone's boyfriend lifted his girlfriend off her feet, spinning her until her cap flew off. Two boys kissed near the bleachers, quick and grinning, and Sierra felt something flicker in her chest that she couldn't quite file away.

She was happy. Genuinely, bone-deep happy. She had her people. She had her work. She had a future that felt real.

But watching those couples walk away—leaning into each other, belonging to someone in that specific, unmistakable way—she noticed the outline of what she didn't have. Not painfully. More like pressing a finger to a bruise just to check if it was still there.

It was.

TWO WEEKS LATER, SIERRA sat in Jonas's studio, surrounded by the glow of editing monitors and the faint smell of coffee that had been reheated too many times.

Jonas leaned over her shoulder, watching her sort through wedding shots.

"You've got instincts, Sierra. You know which images matter."

"I just pick the ones that feel like something."

"That's exactly it."

He pulled up a calendar on his screen. "I want to make this official. Second shooter. Paid hourly plus a cut of the job. You keep learning, I keep booking you."

Her heart stumbled. "You're serious."

"I don't say things I don't mean."

"Yes," she said immediately. "Yes, I'm in."

"Good." He nodded once, decisive. "Also, there's a community center looking for someone to teach beginner photography. Mostly kids. Pay's not glamorous, but it's steady. I recommended you."

"You did?"

"You're patient. You care. Those are more rare than talent."

Sierra blinked rapidly, heat prickling behind her eyes. "Thank you."

"Don't thank me. Just don't waste it."

THAT NIGHT, SHE SPRAWLED on Jett's living room floor with the coven, surrounded by pizza boxes and terrible movie dialogue.

Calliope put her hand on Sierra's shoulder. "Our photographer is becoming famous and will forget us."

"We will haunt her professionally." Raven stared.

Jett nodded. "I expect VIP passes to all future gallery openings."

Sierra laughed, snapping a candid photo of them — Raven mid eye-roll, Jett gesturing dramatically, Calliope already stealing another slice of pizza.

In the frame, everything arranged itself into meaning.

This was what she wanted to do. Capture people when they weren't performing. When they were messy and loud and real.

"What are you smiling about?" Raven asked.

Sierra lowered the camera. "Just thinking... this is it. This is the life I want."

"Wow," Calliope said. "Grossly sincere."

"Tragic," Jett agreed.

But they were smiling, too.

Sierra didn't feel like she was waiting for her life to start. It had already begun — right here, on a living room floor with her best friends and a future that felt both terrifying and possible.

She didn't know where it would lead.

She didn't know what she might lose along the way.

All she knew was that she wasn't alone, and that was enough.

Most days, it was more than enough.

The Room Waiting for Them

Lauren

Before everything changed, Lauren learned that even good beginnings could hurt.

Sometimes the right choice ached. Sometimes leaving a place that saved you felt like betrayal—not because you wanted to stay, but because you had to go, anyway. Love did not always ask you to remain. Sometimes it asked you to leave, to build, to keep moving, and trust that what mattered would survive the distance.

Back then, Lauren was eighteen, packing up a borrowed life that had become home.

Summer After Graduation

The last week at Willow's house moved differently. Time became something she could feel.

Lauren spent their days doing makeup for summer clients—weddings, parties, one sweet sixteen that paid far better than it had any business paying—and their evenings packing, unpacking, and then repacking everything with the anxious conviction that folding a shirt correctly might somehow make adulthood less terrifying.

It did not.

Willow leaned against the bedroom doorframe on Thursday night, arms crossed, watching Lauren refold the same black top for the third time in ten minutes.

"You know that shirt is not going to determine the outcome of your future."

Lauren did not look up. "You don't know that."

"I do, actually. I'm very intuitive."

Lauren sighed and finally set the shirt down. "What if this is a mistake?"

Willow pushed off the frame and crossed the room, dropping onto the bed. "Moving to Brooklyn for a real opportunity in your field is not a mistake."

"What if I can't do it?"

"You can."

"What if I hate it?"

"Then you figure out your next move."

"What if I embarrass myself so thoroughly that Manhattan collectively decides I'm banned from contour forever?"

Willow was quiet for one beat, then said, "That would honestly be iconic, but I still don't think it's going to happen."

Lauren laughed despite themself, then looked down at the half-packed duffel open on the floor.

That was the problem. None of their fear was logical enough to argue with. It was all shape and feeling and memory. The terror of starting over. The old instinct that said safety was temporary, that every good thing had an expiration date stamped somewhere they just hadn't found yet.

Willow's expression softened. "You're going to be fine."

"You keep saying that."

"Because you keep acting like I'm going to suddenly change my answer."

Lauren sat beside the duffel and rubbed their palms against their jeans. "I don't know how to thank you. For any of this. The past two years. Your mom. This room. Everything."

Willow's face did that thing it always did when Lauren got too earnest too fast, equal parts fond and exasperated.

"Stop."

"I'm serious."

"I know." Willow reached over and nudged their shoulder. "You don't thank family for loving you."

The word settled deep. Tender. A little bruised around the edges because Lauren still wasn't fully used to hearing it used without conditions attached.

Family.

Not as leverage. Not as obligation. Not as a threat.

Just love.

J ORDAN CAME OVER THE next night with takeout, three iced coffees no one needed that late in the day, and a playlist titled **Brooklyn or Bust** that she insisted on putting on immediately.

"Subtle," Willow said dryly.

"I believe in setting a tone," Jordan replied, kicking off her shoes and settling onto the floor.

They ate lo mein out of cartons and pretended the night was normal.

Lauren talked about client requests. Willow complained about a woman in her summer literature class who kept calling everything "postmodern" with no clear understanding of what it meant. Jordan spent ten straight minutes ranking the worst wedding speeches she had ever heard, despite only having attended four weddings in her life.

It was ordinary.

Which made it harder.

Because ordinary was exactly what Lauren had once thought they would never get to keep.

At one point Jordan pointed her chopsticks at them and said, "You are texting us when you get there."

"Obviously."

"And after your first GlamSquad job."

"Yes."

"And if your new neighborhood has a weirdly hot barista."

Lauren threw a pillow at her. "I am not moving to Brooklyn to find a hot barista."

"You can build a career and make bad romantic choices," Jordan said. "Women contain multitudes."

Willow nodded solemnly. "That's science."

Later, after Jordan left, and the house quieted, Lauren lay down in the dim glow of Willow's fairy lights and stared up at the ceiling they knew almost by heart.

Two years ago, they had arrived in this room with one duffel bag, a pale blue dress, and enough terror to make breathing feel optional.

They had been grieving. Homeless in every way that mattered. Raw from rejection and too exhausted to imagine anything beyond the next twenty-four hours.

Now they were leaving with a savings envelope tucked in their makeup case, a contract in Manhattan, a room waiting for them in Brooklyn, and a version of themself they had fought hard to become.

Willow's voice drifted through the dark. "You awake?"

"Yeah."

A pause.

"I'm really proud of you."

Lauren swallowed against the tightness in their throat. "I wouldn't be here without you."

"I don't know about that." Willow shifted overhead, the mattress creaking softly. "You would've found a way."

"Maybe." Lauren turned onto their side. "But I'm glad I didn't have to."

That silence again, the comfortable kind.

Then Willow said, very softly, "Me too."

WILLOW'S MOTHER DROVE THEM to Brooklyn on Sunday morning.

Lauren rode in the passenger seat with their makeup kit at their feet and a knot in their stomach that refused to settle. The city thickened as they drove. Streets narrowed, then widened, then filled again. Brick buildings rose shoulder to shoulder. Tree-lined blocks gave way to busier intersections and pockets of neighborhood life that all seemed to move with their own rhythm.

Brooklyn did not feel like Manhattan. Not polished in the same way. Not as sharp-edged. It felt lived in. Layered. Like people built actual lives here instead of just passing through on their way to something more glamorous.

Lauren wasn't sure why that comforted them, but it did.

Aunt Marie's brownstone sat on a quiet block in Park Slope, tucked between rows of stoops with iron railings and flower boxes beginning to droop in the summer heat. She was waiting on the front steps when they pulled up, one hand raised before the car had even fully stopped.

She was in her sixties, maybe, with silver hair pinned back loosely and kind eyes that creased immediately when she smiled.

"Lauren," she said as soon as they stepped out. "It's so good to finally meet you."

Before Lauren could manage more than a nervous hello, Aunt Marie pulled them into a hug that smelled faintly of lavender and something buttery from the kitchen.

It was warm. Uncomplicated. Immediate.

Lauren did not know what to do with that kind of welcome yet.

Inside, the brownstone was all soft afternoon light and old hardwood floors with enough creaks to suggest history. Framed photos covered the walls and side tables, showing birthdays, weddings, holidays, and ordinary Tuesdays turned into keepsakes because somebody had loved the people in them enough to document it.

Aunt Marie led them upstairs to a bedroom at the back of the house.

"It used to be my husband's office," she said, opening the door. "I had some furniture moved in so it would feel more settled."

The room was small but bright, with a narrow bed, a desk by the window, and a view of a tiny garden behind the house where green leaves climbed over a weathered fence.

Lauren stepped inside and just stood there for a moment.

Air. Light. Quiet.

A space that did not feel borrowed, exactly, even if it technically was.

Aunt Marie watched them take it in and smiled gently. "He passed a little over a year ago. The room's been sitting empty ever since. I think he'd like knowing it was being used by someone chasing something they care about."

Lauren set down their bag carefully. "Thank you. Really. I don't want to be a burden."

Aunt Marie waved one hand as if physically shooing the thought away. "No one who worries about being a burden this much ever actually is one."

That earned the smallest laugh out of Lauren.

"Good," Aunt Marie said. "Now let me show you where the towels are, because that's how you know a place is serious about keeping you."

AFTER WILLOW'S MOTHER LEFT, crying just enough to make everyone else start crying too, Lauren unpacked slowly.

Clothes in the dresser.

Brushes and palettes lined up on the desk.

Skincare in the bathroom cabinet.

Phone charger by the bed.

The pale blue dress on a hook behind the door.

That one stopped them for a second.

Not because it hurt, exactly. Maybe because it still did, a little.

That dress had been terror and truth and grief all at once. The beginning of one life ending and another one refusing not to begin.

Lauren touched the fabric lightly, then stepped back.

On impulse, they took out their phone and snapped a photo of the window, the garden, and the rectangle of late afternoon sunlight spilling across the desk.

They posted it with only a short caption.

Day one in Brooklyn. New room. New chapter.

The responses came quickly.

Willow: Already miss you but so excited for you

Jordan: Go be amazing, obviously

@GlamSquadNYC: Welcome to the neighborhood. Your first briefing is Tuesday.

Lauren stared at the last message for a moment longer than necessary.

Tuesday.

Not abstract anymore. Not later. Not someday.

Real.

DINNER THAT NIGHT WAS pot roast, roasted vegetables, and tea afterward at the kitchen table while the sky dimmed outside the windows.

Aunt Marie had the sort of easy conversation style that made silence feel unnecessary but never threatening. She asked about Lauren's work, their plans, whether Manhattan makeup artists were all as intimidating as they seemed on social media.

Lauren laughed and admitted they had no idea yet.

"My husband was a painter," Aunt Marie said after a

while, stirring a little sugar into her tea. "Portraits, mostly. Faces fascinated him."

Lauren looked up. "Really?"

"Oh yes. He said every face tells on the person wearing it if you know how to look."

Something in that made Lauren smile. "That sounds a little like makeup, actually."

Aunt Marie's eyes warmed. "Then I imagine you two would have liked each other."

Later, washing dishes side by side, Lauren found themself thinking about all the artists they had never met and somehow still belonged to. The ones who believed that faces held stories. The ones who spent their lives trying to see people more clearly and help others do the same.

Maybe there was something comforting in that, too. The idea that they were not inventing this path from scratch. That other people had walked strange, creative, uncertain roads before them and still managed to make lives out of it.

T HAT NIGHT, IN THEIR new room, Lauren sat at the desk and looked out at the garden while the last scraps of light disappeared.

Somewhere beyond that dark was the GlamSquad studio. Future clients. Strange subway rides. Early mornings. Long days. Rooms full of people they did not know yet.

A life still waiting to introduce itself.

They opened their laptop and started sketching out content ideas. New tutorials. Product breakdowns. Looks they wanted to try before fall. Ways to keep growing, keep pushing, keep becoming.

Their phone buzzed.

Willow: How's it feel?

Lauren looked around the room before answering. The bed. The desk. The dress. The stillness.

Lauren: Scary. Right. Both.

Willow: That's how you know it matters.

Lauren set the phone down and leaned back in the chair.

Outside the window, the garden had gone dark. But the street beyond it was still alive—someone walking a dog, a car door closing, and then, faintly, a couple laughing together on the sidewalk. The sound drifted up and hung in the air like perfume from a passing stranger.

Lauren listened until it faded.

The room was quiet in a way Willow's room had never

been. No mattress creaking overhead. No soft breathing from someone who'd stayed up too late reading. No presence on the other side of the dark reminding them they weren't alone.

They weren't lonely. That was important to say, even silently. They had Willow a phone call away, Jordan ready to invade tomorrow, a career about to begin. Their life was fuller than it had been two years ago by an almost incomprehensible margin.

But full wasn't the same as complete.

Somewhere in this city, people were falling asleep next to someone who knew how they took their coffee, and which side of the bed they preferred, and what their face looked like first thing in the morning before the day put its mask on.

Lauren wondered what that felt like. Not in the abstract. In the specific, physical, terrifying particular.

For a long time, survival had been the goal. Just make it through. Get safe. Get stable. Don't ask for too much.

But here, in a small room in Brooklyn with a window over a garden and a future waiting two days away, a new thought surfaced.

Safe was no longer the finish line.

It was the starting point.

Lauren closed their eyes for a moment and let that settle.

They had made it through grief. Through rejection. Through fear sharp enough to cut. Through every version of themself that had once believed there would never be a place in the world where they could exist without apology.

Now they were here.

Not finished. Not certain. Not fearless.

But ready.

And the future felt like something they were building toward, on purpose.

It felt like something they were about to walk into on purpose.

The Beginning of Everything

Sierra

Five Years Later

BY LATE AFTERNOON, THE light in Jonas's studio turned honey-soft, pooling across the hardwood floors and catching on the edges of framed prints stacked against the wall. Sierra loved this hour. Everything looked warm. Forgiving. Like the day was quietly apologizing for whatever chaos it had contained earlier.

She capped her lens and leaned back in her chair, stretching until her spine popped.

"Done pretending to work?" Jonas asked from across the room without looking up from his editing monitor.

"I am working," she said. "Strategically."

"You've been staring at the same photo for twelve minutes."

"It's called contemplation."

"It's called procrastination."

She stuck her tongue out at his reflection in the glass of a framed print. Five years later, some things held the same.

The studio was busier than it used to be. Wedding albums stacked in neat towers. Corporate headshots queued for retouching. Modeling assignments. A whiteboard filled with bookings that stretched three months ahead. Jonas had stopped introducing her as his assistant a long time ago. Now she was "my second shooter" or, more recently, "Sierra handles that."

It still startled her sometimes, hearing her name attached to competence.

"Go home," Jonas said finally. "You've been here since eight."

"So have you."

"Yes, but I'm ancient and fueled entirely by caffeine and regret."

She snorted, packing her camera into her bag. "I have plans anyway."

"Big glamorous Friday night?"

"Extremely glamorous," she said. "Community art fair."

Jonas perked up. "Photography?"

"Mixed media. LGBTQIA showcase. One of my students begged me to go."

"Good. Look at other art. It keeps you from becoming boring."

"I was not aware that was a risk."

"It's always a risk."

THE FAIR OCCUPIED A converted warehouse strung with warm lights and draped banners in soft gradients of color. Music drifted through the space, something mellow and acoustic, punctuated by bursts of laughter and the low murmur of conversations overlapping.

Sierra paused just inside the entrance, letting the atmosphere settle around her.

She loved rooms like this. Rooms where nobody expected anything specific from her. No client demands. No timelines. Just people making things because they needed to.

"Miss Sierra!"

She turned to see Ava weaving through the crowd, paint smudged across her cheek like a badge of honor.

"You came!"

"Of course. I said I would."

Ava bounced on her toes. "My piece is over there. But

also there's photography upstairs and this sculpture that looks like it's melting but in a good way."

"Lead the way," Sierra said.

They wandered through displays of paintings, ceramics, fiber art, and digital installations. Ava narrated enthusiastically the entire time, pointing out friends' work, favorite pieces, things she didn't understand but liked, anyway. Sierra listened more than she talked, which was maybe her favorite thing about Ava — the girl could fill a room with genuine excitement and never once make you feel like you were expected to match it.

They had just stopped in front of a large abstract canvas — bold, overlapping strokes of ochre and deep violet — when a familiar voice cut through the crowd noise from behind.

"There's my girl!"

She turned.

Calliope was already moving toward her, red hair sharp and spiky, face lit up. She had a cup of something warm in one hand and a program booklet crumpled in the other. Behind her — and this was the part that required a moment of genuine recalibration — came Jett.

Jett, who had apparently decided in the past few months to become an entirely different structural category of person.

"Jett, you get more muscular every time I see you," Sierra said, before she could stop herself.

He grinned. The sleeveless shirt was doing a lot of work. Or rather, it wasn't doing enough work, because the arms coming out of it were huge.

"You're massive. I knew you were getting buff, but that's incredible."

Jett shrugged like it was obvious. "I go to the gym every day now. No exceptions."

Calliope bumped his arm with her shoulder. "He literally texted me from the gym on Christmas morning."

"The gym was open."

"It was seven a.m."

"Still open."

Sierra looked at him — really looked, the way you do when someone's changed in a way that rearranges some quiet assumption you'd held without realizing it. He stood differently, too. Not puffed up or performative, just solid. Like he'd decided to take up the space he'd always been entitled to.

"Are you okay? Like, is this good." Sierra grabbed his hand.

"It's good." He said it without hesitation. No layered undercurrent, no deflection. "Nobody's going to mess with me the way they used to. Nobody." A beat. Then a smaller smile. "Also, I just really like it. The gym. It makes sense in a way a lot of things didn't."

Ava, who had been watching them with wide, delighted eyes, leaned slightly toward Sierra and whispered, "Is that your friend group? They're so cool."

"They have their moments," Sierra said.

"Rude." Calliope glared at her. She extended a hand to Ava with the easy confidence of someone who'd long since decided strangers were just future friends. "Calliope. You're the student she never shuts up about?"

Ava blinked. "She talks about me?"

"Constantly."

Sierra chose not to confirm or deny this. "Where's everyone else?"

"Mira and Dev are upstairs. Theo is literally standing in front of a ceramic teapot looking like he's going to cry about it, he's been there for ten minutes." Calliope waved vaguely toward the far corner. "I tried to move him along and he said, and I quote, 'not yet.'"

Sierra laughed — real, surprised, fully involuntary. "That is so him."

"We were going to do a full loop," Calliope said, glancing at Ava with an easy, including look. "You all should come with us."

Ava turned to Sierra, practically vibrating. Sierra raised

an eyebrow. "Is that a yes?"

"That is so a yes."

So they went. All of them. Eventually, Theo peeled away from the teapot, Mira and Dev found them upstairs near a photography installation, and somehow the whole chaotic orbit of people Sierra had been carrying through the last five years ended up wandering the same warm, lit warehouse together.

Jett crouched down to get a better look at a low-hung sculpture, and the shirt situation became briefly architectural. Mira caught Sierra's eye across the room and mouthed *what* with appropriate emphasis. Sierra pressed her lips together and looked away.

They were somewhere between the fiber art wall and a series of ink prints when Calliope's phone buzzed. She glanced at it, then looked up with the specific expression of someone not remotely surprised.

"Raven's here."

"Finally," Dev said.

"She said she got stuck on the subway."

"She always gets stuck on the subway."

"She does always get stuck on the subway," Jett agreed.

Three minutes later, Raven materialized out of the crowd — slightly breathless, jacket half-off one shoulder, scanning the room with the focused urgency of someone who had been late to enough things to have perfected the art of arriving like she meant to. She spotted them and her whole face shifted into relief.

"Okay, I'm here, I'm so sorry, the train just sat there for twenty minutes, I was losing my mind." She stopped. Took in the full group. Then Sierra. "Oh good, you made it too. I was worried it was just going to be me showing up and not knowing where anyone was."

"We've been here an hour," Calliope said pleasantly.

"I know, I know." Raven looped her arm through Sierra's with the ease of someone reclaiming a natural place in the order of things.

Ava led them back to the abstract painting they'd been trying to see earlier. Nobody was blocking it now, and she spent four minutes explaining exactly why she thought the bottom left corner was the emotional core of the whole piece. Jett listened with his arms crossed and his head tilted, nodding. "I see it," he said at the end. "I actually see it."

Ava beamed like she'd been handed something.

Upstairs, near the exit, a long corkboard held dozens of business cards pinned in uneven rows. Artists. Tutors. Musicians. Freelancers. People trying to be found.

Sierra slowed.

She had been meaning to make cards for years. Everyone told her she should. Networking. Visibility. Professionalism. Instead, she had a handful of simple ones Jonas had printed for her after she finally gave in.

She pulled one from her wallet, turning it over between her fingers.

SIERRA RIVERA — Photography — Portraits | Events | Creative

Minimal. Clean. Terrifying.

"Put it up," said Calliope, appearing at her shoulder.

"What if no one calls?"

"What if someone does?" Ava put her hand on Sierra's shoulder.

She pinned the card to an open space near the center, pressing the tack firmly into the board.

There. Existing publicly. Horrifying.

Ava grinned. "Look at you, being all official."

"Don't make it weird."

LATER, OUTSIDE, THE EVENING air felt cooler, washed clean by the fading heat of the day. Ava bounced toward her ride, waving until she disappeared into a car, and the coven spilled out onto the sidewalk in the scattered, unhurried way of people who hadn't quite agreed when the night was over.

Mira linked her arm through Sierra's. "Good night."

"Really good," Sierra said, and meant it.

They drifted in separate directions. Theo still talking about the teapot, Calliope already texting, Jett rolling his shoulders back with the unconscious ease of someone who'd recently discovered exactly how much space he was allowed to take up.

Sierra watched him for a moment.

Nobody's going to mess with me the way they used to. Nobody.

She thought about that walk home he'd had once, years ago, shoulders up near his ears. The way he used to go quiet in rooms where he should have been loud.

People changed. Sometimes slowly, and sometimes like they'd simply decided.

L IFE HAD FINALLY SETTLED into something predictable.

Work was steady. Teaching filled her mornings twice a week. The coven still met whenever schedules aligned, which was less often than it used to be but somehow more intentional. Nobody was drifting away. Just growing outward.

Nothing felt like it was on fire.

Nothing was wrong.

And yet there was a hollow place. Not in her career, not in her friendships, not in the life she'd built with such deliberate, stubborn care. A hollow she couldn't photograph.

She adjusted the strap of her camera bag and started walking, not in any particular hurry to get home.

By the time she reached her neighborhood, golden hour had begun its slow descent into dusk. The sky glowed in soft bands of peach and violet — the light photographers chased obsessively, because it made everything look like a memory.

She paused at the corner, looking toward the park.

From here, the trees were only a dark silhouette between buildings, but she knew the paths by heart. She used to wander there constantly with her camera. Lately, not so much. Work shoots had replaced personal ones. Deadlines had replaced curiosity.

Maybe she missed it.

Maybe she missed doing something just because she wanted to.

She imagined the pond catching this light. People walking dogs. Kids chasing each other across the grass. Strangers existing in their own private universes, unaware of being seen.

Real moments. Unposed. Unfiltered.

Her chest tightened slightly. Not pain. Just... unfinished.

Maybe she should stop waiting for permission.

Tomorrow, she decided, she would go.

Early. Before the crowds. Bring the good lens. Photograph whatever caught her eye — people, birds, reflections on the water, anything honest and unscripted.

Something new.

Something that belonged only to her.

Sierra adjusted the strap on her bag and turned toward home, already planning the settings she might start with, the angles she wanted to try, the way the morning light would fall across the paths.

Tomorrow, she'd bring her camera.

She did not know that tomorrow, across a stretch of sunlit water, she would see someone feeding birds and laughing alone, and that her whole chest would go still.

The Beginning of Everything

Lauren

Five Years Later

THE WEEK HAD BEEN brutal.

Three fashion shows in a row. A bride who changed her entire look thirty minutes before walking down the aisle. A photoshoot that ran hours late because the creative director could not decide whether she wanted "sun-kissed goddess" or "ethereal moonlight."

Lauren loved their job. They really did.

But some weeks demanded a recovery period.

By Thursday evening, they found themself wandering through a converted warehouse in Brooklyn, the air warm with bodies and string lights and the low thrum of acoustic music. A banner near the entrance read *Queer Arts Collective — Annual Showcase*.

They had not planned to come. A coworker had mentioned it in passing, said it was good, said there would be wine and people who did not talk about contour palettes as if they were life-or-death decisions.

Mostly, Lauren had come because they were tired of going straight home.

The space was crowded but not claustrophobic. Paintings lined the brick walls. Sculptures occupied islands of floor space. Conversations overlapped in a soft, steady murmur that felt almost like ocean noise.

Lauren moved slowly, hands tucked into the pockets of their oversized cardigan, absorbing color and texture without trying to analyze any of it.

It felt good to be somewhere that did not require performance.

They stopped near a large abstract painting that seemed to pulse with movement, thick layers of color dragged across the canvas as if the artist had been trying to outrun something.

Four people stood directly in front of it, blocking most of the view.

Lauren waited.

One of them was a woman with short, spiky red hair, gesturing animatedly as she talked. Beside her stood a tall, broad-shouldered man with deep ebony skin and arms built like he could carry furniture up three flights of stairs without breaking a sweat. The other two shifted in and out of Lauren's line of sight, voices blending into the ambient noise.

They seemed happy. Loud. Comfortable in a way Lauren still sometimes had to fake.

After a minute, Lauren smiled faintly to themself.

It was fine. There was more to see.

They moved on.

Upstairs, a long corkboard covered one wall near the exit, crowded with business cards pinned in uneven rows. Tutors. Tattoo artists. Freelance designers. Bands looking for venues. People trying to be found.

Lauren scanned them absently.

A photography card caught their eye.

Simple. Clean. Confident.

They reached out, fingertips brushing the edge as if testing whether touching it would obligate them to something. For a moment they imagined having portraits done. Not professional headshots. Something softer. Something honest.

Then practicality intruded. Bills. Groceries. The endless math of adult survival.

Not right now.

They let their hand fall and stepped away.

By Friday evening, they were on the subway with a canvas tote of birdseed in their lap and a headache pulsing behind one eye. Outside the window, Brooklyn blurred past in streaks of brick and graffiti and late-summer light.

Prospect Park meant quiet. It meant space. It meant remembering that the world was bigger than deadlines and fluorescent dressing rooms and the constant hum of being needed.

The ritual had started about a year earlier. One terrible day, they had sat on a bench and watched sparrows dismantle a dropped bagel with ruthless efficiency. Something about it had cracked through the pressure in their chest. The next week they came back with actual seed.

After that, it became habit.

Reset button. Oxygen mask. Proof they could still stop moving.

The park was lively but not crowded. Joggers passed in neon shoes. Someone strummed a guitar under a tree, only mostly in tune. A couple argued quietly over a takeout container. Late sunlight turned everything warm and forgiving.

Lauren headed for their usual bench by the pond.

"Home sweet home," they murmured, dropping onto the wood slats.

They scattered the first handful of seed. Sparrows descended instantly, hopping closer in bold, jittery bursts. One landed on the bench beside them, head cocked as if evaluating their worthiness.

"Yes, I brought snacks." Lauren said softly.

The bird remained unimpressed.

Another handful. Wings fluttered. Tiny bodies bumped into each other with squeaky indignation. It was chaotic, ridiculous, completely unconcerned with anything beyond the present moment.

Lauren felt their shoulders loosen.

Five years ago they had been sleeping on an air mattress, counting coins for groceries, trying to believe survival could turn into something more. Now they had a small apartment, steady work, clients who requested them by name, and friends who showed up without being asked.

It was not perfect. Nothing ever was.

But it was theirs.

Across the park, someone moved with deliberate stillness. A photographer, maybe. Golden hour drew them out like clockwork. Lauren noticed only in passing, more shape than person, a silhouette with a camera lifted to their face.

They looked away. People photographed strangers in parks all the time. It was part of city life. No big deal.

"Share," Lauren told an especially aggressive sparrow

who had claimed a private pile of seeds. "We are building a community here."

The sparrow refused to negotiate.

Their phone buzzed.

Jordan: Are you alive? Willow thinks you died of overwork.

Lauren smiled.

Lauren: Alive. At the park. Feeding birds like someone's eccentric aunt.

Jordan: Honestly that tracks.

Another vibration.

Willow: Love you. Don't forget we're invading tomorrow. Brunch or bust.

Lauren: I will be properly caffeinated and emotionally prepared.

They slipped the phone back into their pocket.

The air smelled like warm grass and pond water and something sweet from a nearby food cart. Children shrieked in the distance. A dog barked at absolutely nothing. The sun lowered until the pond became a sheet of liquid gold.

For a moment, Lauren let themselves do nothing at all.

No planning. No rehearsing conversations. No scanning the future for potential disasters.

Just breathing.

They were not lonely, exactly. Their life was full. Busy. Supported. Loud in all the right ways.

But sometimes—in the subway at rush hour, surrounded by strangers leaning into each other; or at a shoot, watching a couple share a look they thought nobody caught; or here, now, on a park bench with only sparrows for company—their chest loosened. Someone to share this with. Someone to know.

They wanted someone who would sit on this bench beside them and not need to fill the silence. Someone who would notice the way the light hit the water and understand why Lauren couldn't look away. Someone who would see them—not the artist, not the survivor, not the story—just them, tired and real and feeding birds at golden hour because the world got too loud.

They didn't know who that person was.

But wanting it was honest now. Real.

The birds finished the seed and dispersed in a flurry of wings. One lingered on the bench, then darted away too, leaving Lauren alone with the quiet.

They brushed crumbs from their jeans and stood.

The photographer was still somewhere across the park.

Lauren could sense movement without looking directly. Whoever it was seemed focused, patient, waiting for something.

Good for them.

Lauren took one last look at the pond, committing the color of the light to memory. These moments never lasted. That was what made them precious.

Their phone buzzed again.

> **Willow:** Bring pastries tomorrow.

> **Lauren:** Already on it.

She threw the last of the seed in the air as the sparrows swarmed her. She laughed at her feathered friends and turned toward the park exit.

Behind them, the sun dipped lower, outlining everything in a soft halo. The photographer shifted position. A shutter clicked — too far away to hear over the city noise.

Lauren walked on, unaware.

Somewhere behind them, a shutter clicked. A stranger lowered her camera and stood very still, watching the light where Lauren had been.

The photograph would live on that stranger's screen for hours that night, not because it was flawless, but because the person in it mattered.

And tomorrow morning, on a bench by the same pond, two lives that had been building toward each other for years would finally, quietly, collide.

They left through the gate and disappeared into the evening crowd.

Continue the Story

Loving Lauren — *Book One in the Chaos Coven series*

Photographer Sierra Turner has always been better at capturing other people's moments than living her own. Until one afternoon in the park changes everything.

Lauren creates beauty for a living, but they've spent years learning that being seen comes with risks. When their worlds collide, both must decide whether love is worth the vulnerability it demands.

Loving Lauren is a contemporary LGBTQIA+ romance about chosen family, personal growth, and discovering that sometimes the most beautiful love stories begin when you finally stop running from yourself.

Features pansexual and transgender protagonists with themes of family, identity, and healing. A tender, character-driven romance with gentle intimacy and emotional depth.

Read it now: https://www.carlybwrites.com/loving-lauren

Coming Soon

Taming Jett

Book Two — Coming Fall 2026

The story isn't over.

Taming Jett is coming later this year, and this one has been a long time coming. Follow along for updates, cover reveals, and release news.

Stay in the loop: https://link.carlybwrites.com/socials

Also by Carly Bryant

Encore

A Standalone Rockstar Romance Novella

When a broken-hearted animal rescue owner meets a rising country star ten years her junior, sparks fly, but can their connection survive the real world?

Autumn Winters has sworn off men. At thirty-four, she's got enough on her plate running a struggling animal rescue without adding relationship drama. Then she locks eyes with Cole Stone across a crowded bar, and every rational thought vanishes.

He's twenty-four. A musician. Everything she's told herself to avoid.

But Cole sees past her walls, her insecurities, and her dog-hair-covered wardrobe. He wants her... age gap, trust issues, and all.

Three days. That's all they have before his tour takes him away. Three days to decide whether this combustible chemistry is worth the risk.

Because falling for Cole means believing she deserves a second chance at love. It means trusting that someone won't leave when things get hard. And it means figuring out if their different worlds can somehow collide without destroying each other.

Sometimes the best encores are the ones you never saw coming.

Available now: https://www.amazon.com/dp/B0GC V48HDB

About the author

Carly Bryant writes contemporary romance filled with heartfelt emotions, awkward charm, and the kind of love stories that linger long after the last page. Her characters stumble, grow, and learn to love themselves as deeply as they love each other, creating narratives that feel both tender and true.

When she isn't writing, Carly is usually spending time with her husband, three dogs, and countless koi. She's an avid reader with a special love for indie authors.

Follow her at https://link.carlybwrites.com/bryant

https://carlybwrites.com

Or scan the QR code.